DAMIEN

SAN FRANCISCO SHOCKWAVES
BOOK 4

SAMANTHA LIND

SAMANTHALIND.COM

Damien
San Francisco Shockwaves Book 4
Copyright 2023 Samantha Lind
All rights reserved.

Cover Design by *Jersey Girl Design*
Cover image by Wander Aguilar
Cover Model : Zac S
Editing by *Amy Briggs ~ Briggs Consulting LLC*
Proofreading by *Proof Before You Publish*

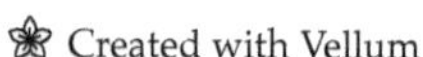 Created with Vellum

CONTENTS

CHAPTER 1
DAMIEN

I sit in the conference room while Coach gives the rundown of camp. It's all information I've heard many times over. I've played in the NHL for sixteen seasons. I'm fucking old for a hockey player at the ripe age of thirty-eight. Add to that the two seasons I played in the minors, and juniors before that. I've been strapping skates to my feet since I was a toddler. Hockey runs in my blood. I honestly don't know what I'd be doing with my life if I didn't play hockey, and it's something my agent keeps pestering me about once it's time to hang up the ole skates. While I have no idea when that day will actually come, I do know that it is sooner rather than later.

I've tuned Coach out a little bit, not really caring what he's saying to all the young guys. I know the drill. Keep my focus on staying healthy and winning games. No distractions.

"I need everyone's attention for another minute," Coach calls out and I look his way. "The front office has created a new position, a social media manager. Specifically, one that will be dealing with connecting fans with the team. These types of social media interactions have become extremely popular with the likes of Tiktok and Instagram, or so I'm told.

It is expected that you will cooperate and interact, as requested, and outlined in your contracts. I'd like to introduce you to Trinity," Coach says as he motions toward the door as it opens. Every guy in this room sits up a little straighter. I take in the woman who enters. She's fucking gorgeous, but also so fucking young, young enough that my dick shouldn't be twitching in my shorts unless I want to get myself in trouble. If I had to guess, I'd say she's in her early to mid-twenties. "I expect all of you to be on your best behavior. Trinity will be with us most of the time, including traveling with us to most away games. I've been told that some of her planned footage won't even require you to do anything extra as she'll be capturing behind-the-scenes footage that fans want more of. But…" he says as he looks around the room, making quick eye contact with most of us before he resumes talking. "If she was to approach you for a short interview, then please participate without giving her any shit."

The guys murmur their agreements to Coach's request. I stay silent. The way I stay most of the time. Some guys think I'm an asshole, but really, I just don't like talking. Some call me broody, or an introvert. I let them label me, because at the end of the day, who fucking cares what other people think of me. I do my job and I don't bother anyone.

I wasn't always like this. I was once an easy-going guy. Had a big group of friends back in Carolina that I hung out with regularly. That all changed eight years ago. I'll never forget the look on my coach's face when I got off the ice that night. The moment my entire life changed in the blink of an eye.

Eight Years Ago

THE FINAL BUZZER SOUNDS AND THE CROWD GROANS. THE HOME team wasn't able to score, even after pulling the goalie for the final minute of the game. I'll give it to them, they got a lot of shots on our goalie, but nothing snuck past him.

Everyone converges on our goalie, giving him the credit he deserves after a hard-fought win. We all make our way off the ice and down the tunnel toward the visitors' locker room. We're headed back home tonight, and I can't fucking wait. I haven't seen my wife, Kelly, in five days, and I can't wait to hold her in my arms again. Maybe try our hand at conceiving that baby we've been trying to have for the last couple of months.

"Damien." Coach calls my name as I leave the bench and head down the tunnel. "A word with you," he says and the hairs on the back of my neck stand up. The look on his face tells me I'm not going to like what he has to say. I flip through all my time on the ice tonight as I follow him down the hall and into a small room that's next to the locker room. He shuts the door before turning to me.

"Did I do something wrong?" I ask, not sure what this might be about.

He shakes his head as he rubs a hand on the back of his neck, squeezing it as if he's attempting to provide relief from the stress he carries there.

"I think you need to sit down," he tells me, and I can't imagine what he's got to say to me that would require me to be sitting.

"Just spit it out, Coach," I grit out. My molars grind together hard, so much so, I'm shocked I don't crack them while I wait for him to spit out whatever it is that he needs to say.

A few seconds tick by and he isn't saying anything, so I sit down on the chair behind me.

"We got a call about ten minutes ago from the police department. Kelly was struck by a semi on the highway that lost control and she didn't make it. I'm so sorry, Damien." My entire world goes silent as it comes crashing down.

"No, no, no." I stand quickly, not believing what he's just told me. "She can't be gone, I just talked to her this afternoon," I tell him as I reach for the door. I need to get out of here and to my phone. I have to call her.

"I'm so sorry, Damien," he says as I go running from the room and into the locker room to find my stuff. I don't even comprehend what is going on around me as my teammates are all in different stages of taking their gear off and getting ready to hit the showers. I make it to my stall and start ripping my bag apart searching for my phone. When I finally find it, I see multiple missed calls from unknown numbers, and a few of them have left me messages, so I click on the first one, listening to it.

"Mr. Thompson, this is Dr. Carr, I need to speak with you as soon as possible. Please call me back at this number, it will come directly to me. It is extremely important that I speak with you as soon as possible." His words hardly register as my ass hits the bench and my world continues to crash down around me. I tap the next message, and this time a woman's voice fills my ears. "Mr. Thompson, this is Officer Base, I need to speak with you regarding your wife, Kelly Thompson, please call me back at your earliest convenience."

My phone hits the ground, along with my tears. I don't know how long I sit there in that locker room and sob. I reach for my phone, wiping the moisture from my face, and hit the doctor's number. When I look up, I notice the locker room is quiet, the faces all around me looking somber as they go about their night, knowing that they'll be returning to their wives and girlfriends. I'll be returning to a living hell. One I was never prepared for.

"Hello," I greet, my voice rough from the emotion coursing through my body. "This is Damien Thompson; I'm returning Dr. Carr's call."

"Hello, Sir, this is Dr. Carr. Thank you for getting back to me. I've been informed the police were able to track down someone with your team to relay the devastating news. I'd like to give you my condolences and assure you we did everything we could to save your wife."

"Thank you. Did she suffer?" I ask, not really sure what else to say.

"No, she was unconscious when brought in and never regained consciousness in the time she was in the ER. She was declared brain dead within thirty minutes of arrival. She's currently on a ventilator to keep her organs alive, but no brain functions have been recorded. We want to confirm with you that Kelly is a registered organ donor, and that you approve with us moving forward with that process?"

"Yes, is she able to donate? I know that was important to her. She has a cousin who received a kidney when they were younger."

"As long as we can get her into the operating room soon, we can safely donate many of her organs and tissues. I can alert the team while I have you on the phone so they can get the paperwork started. Do you have any questions for me, at this time?" he asks.

"I should be back in town in a few hours. Will I be able to see her when I arrive?"

"Since she's currently on a ventilator, we will wait to start surgery until our transplant teams have things set up, usually within a few hours, at most. I can delay them until after you've arrived and had a chance to say your goodbyes."

"Can her family come into town, as well?" I ask, racking my brain on if it is even possible to get them there that quickly.

"It's possible, but also dependent on how the body and organs respond to the ventilator and medication we use to keep the body alive until that time. If the organs start to shut down, they are no longer viable for donation. It is a very fine line we have to walk, but we also want to respect your wishes," he explains.

"I'll get them there as soon as possible, and I'll head straight there after the flight touches down."

"You can ask for me at the main ER check-in desk. I'll let them know to page me right away. Better yet, call me or send me a text when you land so I know you're on your way and I'll do my best to be waiting for you when you arrive."

"Thank you," I tell him before we disconnect. I immediately hit the contact for my father-in-law.

"Damien, I didn't expect a call from you tonight. What a hell of a game. You looked good out there."

"Thanks, David," I say, my voice back to being gruff with the emotion lacing it. David and I go way back. He was my head coach when I played juniors and is the reason I even met Kelly.

"What's wrong?" he asks.

"Kelly," I whisper as a sob escapes.

"Kelly what? You're scaring me here, Damien."

"She's gone," I tell him. "I need you guys to get to Raleigh as soon as possible. They're keeping her on a vent until we can say our goodbyes, then taking her into surgery for organ and tissue donation as per her wishes."

"What?" he gasps. "She's gone?" he repeats.

"I don't know much, just that she was in a car accident," I tell him, wishing that I knew more…or hell, that it was me in that hospital bed hooked up to the vent.

"I'll get us there; I take it you're still in Buffalo?"

"Yeah, still in all my shit. Coach pulled me aside as soon as I came off the ice and gave me the news."

"Fuck, I don't even know what to say," he says earnestly.

"Make that two of us," I tell him. "I need to go shower and get to the bus so I can get on that flight back. I need to see her."

"Call me if you need me. I'll let you know when we should arrive."

"Thanks, talk soon," I tell him before I end the call.

I strip from my gear, numb from the pain and emotion coursing through my veins. I gather my shower bag and towel and head for one of the open bays. The room stays quiet, guys murmuring amongst themselves as they finish getting ready to leave.

"I'm so sorry for your loss, please let us know what we can do for you," Johnny, our team captain, says to me once I'm dressed in my suit.

"Thanks, man. I don't even know what to say right now. Just numb over the news."

"I can't even begin to understand what you're going through, but just know we're here for you."

Every guy on the team takes turns pulling me into a manly hug, giving me their love and comfort before we head back home where I must deal with this tragedy head on.

Present Day

"All right, I want everyone on the ice in twenty minutes," Coach calls out, bringing my attention back to the present. I have no idea what I just missed while the memories of that dreadful day came rushing back like they were just yesterday. The pain of losing Kelly doesn't ever go away, but it's slowly becoming easier to live with.

CHAPTER 2
TRINITY
THREE WEEKS AGO

I CHECK MY EMAIL ONCE AGAIN AND I'M DUPED WHEN A NEW one pops up, only to promise me a million dollars from some Nigerian prince if I send them two thousand dollars for a processing fee. No thank you. Who even falls for this kind of shit?

I was so hopeful I'd get something on the job I interviewed for last week. The HR lady assured me they were making decisions and sending out notifications by end of business today. I checked the clock once again just as I hit the refresh button on my email. It is only five after two, so they still have plenty of time before it's the end of the workday.

The position would be for the newest team to join the NHL, the San Francisco Shockwaves, as their newest social media manager and photographer. It's like this position was created just for me. It combines all my favorite things; photography, sports, and social media. I couldn't have dreamed up a better position.

I close out the app for my email, forcing myself to open up my editing software and get to work on some images from a baseball game I was hired to cover last night.

I get engrossed in editing the best ten images from the

night, so I can send those over today for some promotional posts the marketing team is working on. Since I contract with this team on a game-by-game basis, they handle all the posting when they see fit. I just provide them with edited images ready to be used.

I check the time again and see that almost two hours have passed; surely, I've received an email by now, so I open the app back up. I've received ten emails in that amount of time, nine of which are all junk. My heart skips a beat when I see the one I've been waiting for since last week.

To: Trinity Black
 From: San Francisco Shockwaves

Hello Ms. Black.

Thank you for your patience as we made our decision on who would best fit within our organization and into the open position.
 I'm honored to offer the Social Media Manager position to you. I've attached the offer letter, along with a summary sheet that goes over all the additional benefits that come with the position. Please take the weekend to look over all these documents. I'm available to touch base on Monday at your earliest convenience. Please feel free to reach out to me via email at any time between now and then if you have any questions.

Sincerely,
 Marsha

I RE-READ THE EMAIL THREE MORE TIMES BEFORE LETTING OUT THE loudest scream I think I've ever let out. I give myself a minute to freak out before I open the attachments and start reading over the offer and benefits.

I'm blown away by the offer; they were not playing

when they put together this employment package. I don't even know if it is necessary for me to counter on anything. The salary is very generous, as are the retirement, health insurance, and time off compensation. Not to mention the budget for equipment needed to perform the job as assigned.

I tap the screen of my phone, bringing up the contact for my best friend, Michael.

"Hey, girl!" he says, drawing out the first word in his comical way.

"Guess what?" I practically screech.

"What?" He matches my enthusiasm.

"I got the job!" I tell him as I read over the contract once again.

"You're shitting me?!" he gasps.

"I'm as serious as a heart attack," I say as I do a little happy dance that he can't even see.

"I knew you'd get it! They are lucky to have you on their staff." He's the best hype friend ever. "We should go out and celebrate. Matteo is working nights, so it'd just be the two of us," he says, referring to his husband, who's an anesthesiologist at a local hospital.

I glance at the clock. "I can be ready in half an hour."

"Give me forty-five and I'll be there to pick you up," Michael says.

"Perfect! I can't wait."

The phone rings in my ear twice before my dad answers.

"Hey, Daddy," I greet him.

"How's my favorite daughter doing?" he asks. This is his funny little spiel he does every time I call. Seeing as how I'm his *only* daughter, I know I'm his favorite.

"I'm doing really well, is Mom home? I have some news I wanted to share with both of you at the same time."

"She is. Hold on, I'll get her," he says and I can tell he's pressing the phone to his shoulder like he usually does. "Barbara," he calls, "Trinity is on the phone, needs to talk to both of us."

"I'm coming, Fred," I hear her holler back at him. He must have put me on speakerphone.

"Hi, Honey, glad you called. It feels like we haven't talked in ages," my mom says.

"It was just last week," I remind her.

"Might as well have been a month," she says.

"So, what's your exciting news?" Dad asks.

"Remember that job that I was telling you about?"

"The one with the sports ball team?" Dad asks.

"Hockey team, but close enough." I chuckle. "Well, I just got an email with an employment offer, and it is amazing!" I tell them.

"That's wonderful, Honey," my mom compliments me. "Does this mean you're staying in San Francisco and not moving home anytime soon?"

"Yes, Mom. It means I'm staying here," I tell her. Not that I had any plans to move back.

"I'm happy for you, Kid," Dad says.

"Thanks, this was a big opportunity. I think it will be a great step forward in my career."

"They'll pay you enough to live out there?" Mom asks. She always worries that I'm not going to find a job to support myself.

"More than enough. Their offer is higher than what I even imagined. So much so that I'm not sure if I even need to counter to ask for more."

"That's great to hear, Honey," Mom admits.

"Maybe the two of you can come up and visit once the season has started. Watch a game in person."

"That sounds like fun. Send us the schedule and we can plan a little trip up for a long weekend or something," Dad says.

"Perfect. All right, I need to go jump in the shower. I'm

going to dinner with Michael to celebrate and I need to get ready. I love you both!" I tell them before we disconnect.

Once off the phone, I head straight for my bathroom. I strip down and take the fastest shower I've taken in a long time.

I dance and sing along to a Spotify playlist I saved a while ago that I love to listen to when getting ready. I'm just adding the final touches to my makeup when my phone pings.

MIKEY

I'm here, want me to come up?

TRINITY

I'll be down in a minute!

I take one last look at myself in the mirror, then grab my small purse that has my keys and the essentials and head out the door. After I lock up, I add my keys and my phone to my bag and make my way down the stairs and outside to the parking lot.

"Girl, you look fine tonight!" Michael says, giving me a once over as I slide into the passenger seat of his SUV.

"You like?" I ask as I lean over the center console to kiss his cheek.

"Girl, if I swung your way, I'd be trying to take you home tonight," he says, and I just laugh at his antics.

"Maybe you can be my wingman tonight and help me find a man to go home with," I flippantly suggest.

"No, no, Girl. You need to keep your ass single. Snag you one of them hot hockey boys you'll be working with soon."

"I don't think that's going to happen. I'm sure they have a no fraternization policy," I tell him.

"Well, that's no fun. Think of all the naughty places you could sneak away together." He smiles big.

"It's for the best. I don't need distractions while I'm at work," I tell him as we pull out of the parking lot and onto the busy street. "Where are we going to celebrate?" I ask as Michael drives us.

"Your favorite place," he says nonchalantly.

"How? It usually takes weeks for a reservation!" I exclaim.

"I have my ways." He flashes a huge smile my way quickly before turning his attention back onto the road.

"I love you; I love you; I love you," I chant.

"I know, you can pay me back by naming your firstborn after me," he says, and it is our long-running joke we've had for as long as I can remember.

We chat about his work and what I'm looking forward to the most with this new position I've been offered while he maneuvers us through Friday night traffic in San Francisco. It can quickly become gridlock, so I'm thankful when we finally arrive in the area my favorite little Italian restaurant is located. Michael is lucky and we snag a parking spot on the street just as someone else is pulling out.

The weather is so pleasant tonight that we're seated outside on the patio. The slight breeze that is coming off the bay feels good. We order a couple appetizers to share, along with our first round of celebratory drinks.

"I need some advice," I say once our server has left our table.

"Let me hear it," Michael states, giving me his full attention.

"The employment offer is very generous, not only in my salary amount, but the benefits that come with it, as well. I know the advice is you should never accept the first offer a new employer gives you, as there is always wiggle room. My question is, do you think that is always the case and what should I do? I'm very happy with the offer as it stands."

He places his chin in the palm of his hand of the arm that is resting on the edge of the table. I can tell he's pondering my question. "Hmm, that's a tough one. It's salary, right, not hourly?"

"Correct, since I'm expected to be at the rink during practices, probably before and after sometimes, as well as the games, and it said the majority of road trips. I'll probably clarify that when I speak with HR on Monday, but I'm guessing that means I can only miss a handful of them, I'm sure."

"Sounds reasonable. My advice is to go back and ask for ten grand more a year. The worst they can say is no, but more than likely they'll counter around five thousand more."

"Asking for that much won't make me seem desperate, will it?"

"Not at all, like you've already said, they are going to expect you to counter their offer. They have more money in their budget to hire you."

"Okay, thank you," I tell him. Our server arrives with our drinks and the two appetizers we ordered.

"Sorry about that wait, our bartenders are slammed at this time of night," the young guy tells us.

"No problem, we're just out celebrating my girl, here," Michael says to the server.

"Please don't hesitate to flag me down if you need something else. Were you ready to order dinner tonight?"

We both rattle off our orders. I don't even need to look at the menu before telling him what I want.

"Don't look now, but there is a table full of hot guys just over your shoulder. Maybe you should bump into them on our way out," Michael suggests as he finishes his slice of cheesecake.

"What happened to wanting me to find a hot hockey player?" I smirk at him.

Our server arrives just at that moment. "Oh, Honey, that table is full of hot hockey players." I glance over my shoulder at this table. They aren't wrong, they are pretty hot. And now I have to wonder what team they play for. Is it a possibility they will be my co-workers in a few weeks?

"How do you know that?" I ask our server.

"I pride myself in knowing who all the hot athletes are in this town, especially the ones that frequent my workplace. They tend to be good tippers. Especially when they have women with them," he says.

"Ah, so I take it none have indicated they swing your way?"

He frowns and looks their way longingly. "No signs yet." He almost pouts.

"I promise the right person will come along," Michael tells him. "I married a doctor. Besides his crazy hours at the hospital, I wouldn't exchange him for anyone."

"I love that for you." He pats Michael on the shoulder. "Did either of you need anything else tonight?"

"Just the check, please," I tell him.

"One or are we splitting it tonight?"

"Just one," Michael tells him and winks at me. "Matteo's treat." He smirks as he pulls his credit card out of his wallet.

"I love that man." I sigh. "When is his next weekend off? I think we're due for a boozy brunch."

"He's off next weekend, and I think you're right. I'll get us reservations for next Saturday morning."

"Have I told you lately that I love you?"

Michael looks at his watch before looking back at me. "It's been at least an hour, so you're right on time."

We both laugh at this stitch we have. Our server returns with the check, but before he can even set it down, Michael hands over his credit card to pay for everything.

"I'll be right back with this," the server says before stepping away to run his card and bring the receipt back.

Once on the road, Michael turns down the radio. "I just want you to know how proud I am of you. You went after your dream job and nailed it. I can't wait to see how you excel in it."

"Thank you, it is still surreal that I'm going to be working for a professional hockey team full-time."

"Did the contract say anything about you doing your side contract jobs?"

"No, but with the salary they are offering, I won't need those jobs to make sure I can pay rent and feed myself every month. But I might ask, just for clarification, because in the months that they aren't playing, I might go crazy doing nothing."

"Is the position only during the season?" he asks.

"The salary says it is yearly, so I'm not one-hundred percent sure yet. The email said for me to take the weekend to look over anything and to call on Monday to discuss, so I'm going to look over it again tomorrow and make my list of questions, so I don't forget anything once I'm on the phone with them."

"That's a great plan. If you want me to look over it with you, I'm happy to do so."

"I might take you up on that, but I'll let you know for sure."

Michael drops me off at home. I'm still on cloud nine as I make my way inside and drop down onto my bed. The events of the past few hours are still sinking in.

CHAPTER 3
DAMIEN

I skate around the ice, shaking my legs out as I do so until Coach blows his whistle and skates over near the benches. He's got his whiteboard attached to the glass and a dry erase marker in hand.

He goes over some plays he wants us to work on once we've finished with our normal warm-up drills. Once he's done calling out his instructions, we all head to our spots on the ice to start. Out of the corner of my eye, I catch movement in the stands near the glass. Our practices aren't open to the public at this point, sometimes local media will come out to catch some footage for a story, but that's usually it. The dark, curly hair catches my eye and I realize that it is the girl Coach introduced us to the other day. I can't remember her name, but fuck does she look hot.

"You good, man?" Tristan, my defensive partner, asks as he skates up behind me.

I just grunt, bringing my eyes back to the ice and off the photographer in the corner snapping pictures of us practicing. "How was your summer?" I ask.

"Pretty damn good. Missed your broody ass," he teases me.

"Fuck off," I tell him.

"Let's pick it up," Coach calls out. "None of this sloppy skating I'm seeing."

"You ready?" I ask Tristan. "Let's show up these rookies, show them what it means to play with the big boys."

"I like the way you think," he says and taps my shins with his stick. We take off, showing off our skills on the ice. Feeling the glide of my skates on the ice brings a calmness to my veins. It's the one thing that always brings me back to center. My vice that I don't know how I'll ever give it up. Hockey was my life before Kelly and was what I turned to even more after she died.

"All right, showoffs." Coach chuckles after Tristan and I finish the drill. "Way to make an impression for the young guns."

"At your service, Coach," Tristan jokes with him.

Practice is a ringer, but so much fun. I'm drenched in sweat when we head off, and probably lost five pounds, but it's put me back in my happy place, and for that I'm grateful.

"WHAT ARE YOU DOING TONIGHT?" TRISTAN ASKS AS WE'RE finishing up in the locker room.

"Nothing, just grabbing some food and watching TV."

"Why don't you come over? A few of the guys are also coming."

I ponder his invitation. He's invited me so many times and I give in every once in a while. I always have a good time, but I'm also so used to just being a recluse.

"Come on, man; we don't bite. Kendra has a whole menu prepared for tonight." Just the mention of his wife's cooking has my mouth watering. I was able to snag a few of the meals she offers from her business last season, and they were some of the best things I'd eaten since Kelly was alive.

"Gotta bring Kendra into this, that's low, man. Using your wife to seal the deal."

"Hey, a man knows when he's got a good thing." He smiles. I remember what it was like to smile freely like that when I'd talk about Kelly with the guys.

"Fine, I'll stop by, but only because she's cooking."

"Whatever it takes. We need to get you out of your shell. Get you living a little." He smacks me on the back, and we head for the door. "Be at my place by five thirty."

I just nod in agreement as I grab my own things and head for the door myself.

I make it home about twenty minutes later. I look around my condo and realize just how bland it is. You can tell a bachelor lives here. It's all dark wood and leather furniture, a big ass tv. The only pictures I have are of Kelly and me from our years together. I can't stand to part with them. My bedroom is just as bare. A king-size bed is in the center with end tables on either side. I have another large TV mounted on the wall in here and that rounds out the bedroom. I don't require much. My closet is full, between all the suits I own for game days, to the workout clothes I need to keep in shape.

I check the time; I've got two hours before I'm supposed to be at Tristan's place. I consider what I should do between now and then and settle on a walk outside. Some fresh air will do me some good.

I grab my running shoes and get them laced on. Days like today make me wish I had a dog, but my schedule doesn't allow me to have animals. My travel schedule during the season wouldn't be fair to a dog. They'd have to be boarded so much of the time. Maybe once I retire, I can get one.

I head out into the sunshine. It's a beautiful fall day here, some say it is the best time to visit the area, and I have to agree. I walk the short distance to the walking path. I wasn't the only one with this idea, as the trail is busy today. I pop in my ear buds and turn up the music, walking until I reach the turn around point, then make my way back. I keep a ball cap pulled down, and sunglasses on. I didn't notice anyone recognizing me, so if they did, they didn't bother me. I don't mind when fans ask for an autograph, it is actually really humbling that people know who I am and want a few minutes of my time, but it can also be really inconvenient, at times.

Once home, I grab a quick shower before heading to Tristan and Kendra's place. I stop on my way and grab a bottle of wine, figuring that is an appropriate gift to arrive with. I gravitate toward the brand that was Kelly's favorite. I bought it many times over the years and is my go-to when needing to gift something.

"Holy shit, you actually came," Kendra greets when she opens the door for me.

"I'm here in the flesh," I tell her as I lean down to kiss her cheek and hand over the bottle of wine.

"Has hell frozen over?" Ryker calls out as I walk in.

"Funny," I deadpan and give him my trademark stare.

"Good to see you here, man. You know you're always welcome to come out more," Ryker says as he pulls me into a man-hug.

I grunt. "I'll try," I tell him as we pull apart. I really mean what I said. It's time that I make some changes in life, and putting myself out there more is something that I can do.

I hang out with my teammates and their families. I sit back at one point and it hits me just how much of life I've been missing out on. Most of the guys here, Ryker, Aiden, and Tristan, are all married and have kids. Only Blake, our goalie, and myself are single and living the bachelor life.

"Are you ready for the season?" Blake asks as we both nurse a beer out on the deck.

"Absolutely. You?" I ask.

"Yep, I have a good feeling about this season," he says, and the confidence in his words builds my confidence in this upcoming season.

"Good to hear. How's the hip doing?" I ask him.

"Better than ever. I did a bunch of conditioning over the summer. Really worked on my flexibility, and I feel the strongest I've ever felt, if you can believe that."

"That's great, I look forward to seeing you between the pipes. Making all those hotshots cry when you shut them out."

"Something like that." He chuckles. "What'd you do this summer?" he asks.

"Took some time to relax, then hit the gym hard. Takes a little more for me to keep this old body in game shape."

"That's right, you are getting old," he teases.

"Fuck off," I reply and realize I'm smiling, something I've been doing a lot tonight. I guess I really did need this time out of the house. I take another swig of my beer, finishing it off.

Kendra, Avery, and Tori all make their way out onto the deck and head my way. That's never a good sign when all three descend on me at one time. They must be up to something.

"Damien." Kendra says my name all sweetly.

I grunt in response.

"Aww, it's grumpy Damien," Avery teases.

"Did you expect anything different?" Ryker asks his wife.

"What do the three of you want?" I ask, bracing for what they're going to ask.

"Why do you think we want something?" Tori asks, her eyebrow raising in question as she pins me with her stare.

"In my experience, I'm only ever approached by the WAGS, especially in a group, when they want something from me."

"Damn, he's got us pegged," Avery mutters.

"Maybe you ladies shouldn't have all pounced at once," Aiden calls out to the women.

"Hush, husband," Tori hollers back to him.

"Don't hush me," he shouts back, but you can tell he

doesn't mean it in a malicious way. His tone is completely teasing.

"You won't be saying that later tonight," she quips right back at him, as all the guys cackle at their sparring.

"Can we cut the foreplay until y'all aren't right in front of us, and get back to what it is you wanted when you descended on me," I ask, bringing everyone's attention back to me.

"We have a question for you," Avery starts out.

"Really, I would have never guessed," I deadpan and roll my eyes at them.

"Don't be an ass," Kendra chides.

"I don't think he knows how to be anything but," Tristan calls out and I flip him the bird.

"Y'all are a bunch of assholes, no wonder I only come out once a season." I laugh as all their faces fall. "I'm just kidding."

"Anyway, back to our question," Avery says, then everyone listens up. "We're heading up a charity event this season to benefit the children's hospital. We have a few different events planned. We want to know if you'd be willing to be auctioned off for a date?"

"Are you serious?" I groan. I don't want to let these women down by saying no, but that sounds like my worst nightmare.

"It's for a good cause," Tori says.

"I'm sure it is. Can I just donate some cash, signed jersey, some tickets?" I ask.

"We'll take all of that, but we also want you," Kendra states. "Single women will go crazy over the opportunity to bid on a date with you."

I groan and let my head fall back against the chair. "Why me? Why not Blake or one of the other single guys on the team?"

"Oh, don't worry, we'll be cornering them in the coming

weeks." Avery smirks.

"Y'all married a bunch of vultures," I call out to the guys. "No wonder you all fell so quickly."

"Does that mean you'll do it?" Avery asks and I can hear the anticipation in her question.

"When is this event?"

All three women squeal in excitement before answering my question. "It is December fifteenth. The red carpet will be at five, followed by a cocktail hour, main dinner, and auction. There is a live auction and a silent one going on all night, as well. And before you ask, it isn't a game night, and you don't have one the next day, either."

I grumble to myself, but know I can't tell these ladies no, especially when all the money is going to a children's charity. "Fine, I'll do it, but—" I pause and look at all three women with a stern face, "I get to set the rules for the date. I'll take the winner for coffee. No longer than an hour. We'll meet at the location of *my* choice, at a time that is convenient for *my* schedule. Nothing else."

"Whatever you want, we will make it happen," Avery says cheerily as she claps her hands.

"I'm serious. This isn't an opportunity to set me up with someone, nor is it a chance for some puck bunny to get me to take her home."

"We won't be able to control who bids and wins, but we can do all we can to make it apparent what the auctioned date will include. My suggestion is, between now and then, you come up with three dates and times that will work with your schedule that we can include, that way bidders know ahead of time if it will work for their schedule."

"I can do that," I agree.

"Perfect!" Tori states.

"All right, you ladies got what you wanted, now leave the poor man alone," Tristan comes to my defense.

"They aren't that bad," I admit to him once the women move along from pestering me.

"I didn't know they were going to corner you like that, but I am glad you made it out. Maybe you should try it a few more times this season," he suggests.

"Maybe," I reply. "I think I'm ready to start getting out more," I tell him honestly.

"Anytime you need a place to go, you know you are always welcome here. I mean that," Tristan says as he holds out his beer bottle for me to clank mine against.

I take a long pull from the cold beer. I don't drink many of these once the season starts, so I'm savoring the cold beverage as it slides down my throat. "I appreciate that. I'm sorry I've been such a hermit the last few years."

"Don't sweat it, man. It's just part of your charming personality." He snorts as he takes another swig of beer. Kendra walks back over with Olivia, their infant daughter, and hands her over to Tristan. I watch as he takes the small child in his arms and cuddles her to his chest. His lips fall to the top of her head as he presses a kiss there. Watching him makes me wonder what it would have been like to do the same thing to my own child. What it would have been like to watch Kelly grow throughout her pregnancy, what foods she would have craved at all hours of the night. "Want to hold her?" Tristan asks and pulls my attention back to the here and now.

"Umm," I stammer, and I can feel my palms clamming up.

"She doesn't bite." He chuckles at my apparent discomfort.

"Sure," I finally say as I set my beer bottle down on the ground and hold my hands out for him to pass me the baby. I take Olivia into my hands, not exactly sure how to hold her. She starts babbling as she settles into my lap. "Hi, Olivia," I say to her. What in the hell do you say to a baby that can't talk back.

"The puck bunnies would go wild if they could see this," Kendra says. I look up from the baby and notice all three women have gathered back around not far from me, their phones out and facing this direction.

"Y'all are worse than the paps," I joke with them.

"Your soft side is safe with us. We promise to just keep these memories for our own use," Tori says. I know none of them would do anything with the pictures and video, so I turn my attention back to the baby in my arms and find myself smiling down at the cute little thing as she makes some baby noises and tries stuffing her entire fist into her mouth.

CHAPTER 4
TRINITY

I LOOK AT ALL THE NEW EQUIPMENT THAT WAS DELIVERED THIS morning. Everything on my wish list, they bought. I'm still in shock.

I grab a couple of the lenses, place them in a carrying bag I can wear around my waist, and head to catch the guys as they enter the practice rink.

I find a place to sit down where I can see them coming from a long enough distance so I can get good images. It only takes about five minutes before the first few start to trickle in. Most give me big smiles once they notice me. Since it is a practice, they are all strolling in, clothed in workout clothes and not the suit-and-tie look we are used to seeing them in on game days.

"Morning. Trinity, right?" Ryker, the team captain, asks as he sees me.

"Yes, good to see you this morning." I smile up at him.

"If anyone gives you crap, let me know and I'll set them straight."

"Will do. Can I call you captain?" I ask before he walks away.

"Sure can, most of the guys call me that."

"Sounds good," I tell him as I bring my camera back up and snap some pictures and short video clips of the group of guys currently walking down the hall. I don't know all of them yet, but I also know that not all of the guys here right now will make the final roster. After I got the job offer, and officially accepted it, I started studying the main roster of guys that were on the website. I've also done some stalking to see who is active on social media. I've got a little question-naire for them to fill out so I know who is okay with being tagged in any posts we make on the team's pages.

As soon as everyone has made it into the building, I head back up to my office and start downloading all the images and videos I took. I select a dozen of my favorites and start editing them, then get them posted. The comments start rolling in within seconds of posting. Most are positive; fans who are excited for the new season to start after the few months of no hockey.

I replace my memory card in my camera, and this time grab one of the drones that I can use to get footage from above the action. I head for the practice rink and find a good spot to take a few distance images, then get the drone up into the air. I fly it over the rink, capturing some fun moments before it must catch the eyes of the players, who all look up. I can't help but laugh as they all start waving at it, giving me some excellent footage to use later.

I've interrupted practice enough with the drone, so I bring it down, then head to the glass so I can get some closer shots of the guys as they run drills and plays as the coaching staff calls out instructions to them.

Once satisfied I have enough footage from the ice, I head back to my office, once again to get editing and scheduled posts for the rest of the day. Once I have all of the posts done, I get my forms ready for the guys to fill out.

I walk down to the lower level, where all the locker rooms, weight rooms and other team facilities are located. I find the head coach, Brett Jackson, in the video room watching film as he controls the speed of it so he can watch the exact movement of the players as they go through the plays he was calling out.

I knock on the doorframe, alerting him to my presence. "Do you have a minute, Coach?" I ask.

"Of course, come on in," he says as he pauses the video.

"Did you get everything you need today, Trinity?"

"I got some great footage. The fans are going crazy over what I've already posted online from today."

"Good, good."

"I have a form I was hoping I could have the guys fill out. I want to make sure I have permission to tag their personal accounts when we post from the team's social media accounts."

"Of course. They'll all be in here within the next ten minutes if you want to hang around. You can explain what you need and then I can make sure you get the forms by tomorrow morning, if that works for you."

"That's perfect," I tell him. "I also wanted to apologize about the disruption at practice earlier."

"You're all good. I got a good chuckle out of it."

"The footage was great. I'm going to use it in my mini-camp documentary video."

"Sounds like a good use for it."

"I did a video like it for a baseball team I've worked with in the past and it was a huge hit."

"Might as well give the fans what they want." He chuckles as a few guys start filing into the room. I know many people would kill to have my job. Having unrestricted access to an entire team of professional athletes is pretty cool, if I do say so myself, especially being a woman in my position. I clamp down on my nerves, knowing that, shortly, I'll be speaking to a room full of guys.

"Before we jump into video from today, Trinity needs your attention for a few minutes," Coach tells the room at large.

"Thanks, Coach," I say as I nod in his direction. "Thank you for the great footage today, the fans are already clamoring for more. Before we get further into camp, and then the season, I'd like to make sure I have everyone's personal accounts and whether you'd like posts tagged for you. It doesn't matter one way or the other to me; I want to know what you each want. I'll be leaving these forms here for you to fill out and return to me. I'll take care of the rest. If you have someone that manages your social media pages for you, please include their information and I can make sure they get content of you to post, if you want what I capture for personal use."

"I expect the forms to be completed and turned in before you hit the ice tomorrow morning," Coach tells the guys.

They collectively agree as the stack of forms is passed around the room. "Thanks for your time," I say before stepping aside. I can't let the opportunity go, and I pull my camera out of my bag and snap a few pictures of the team as they sit around the room. Once the forms are all distributed, Coach captures their attention by starting to review the video from their practice. I stay for a little bit, taking some more footage for the documentary and other behind-the-scenes posts I can always use footage for.

"So, how was your first week?" Michael asks as he hands me a drink.

"It was so good. I've gotten so much amazing footage!"

"That's awesome, Sweetheart," Matteo says as he joins us in the living room, a large charcuterie board in his hands that he sets down on the coffee table in their very stylish condo.

"Have you picked out who you'd like to bang in the locker room yet?"

I almost spit out the drink I just took, but manage to get it down without choking on it. "No." I laugh. "Although, I won't lie, they are sure pretty to look at," I tell my two best friends.

"I'm sure they are, especially all sweaty and in skimpy clothes. All those jock straps. Damn, I want your job," Michael says.

"I'm sitting right here." Matteo scoffs. I know they're just joking, seeing as how they are very happily married, but it's still fun to watch the banter between the two of them.

"Honey, you know you're my favorite human on this earth besides Trinity. But a man can still drool over the hot hockey boys."

Matteo rolls his eyes at his husband as he fills his plate with some finger foods off the charcuterie board. I do the same before I show them some of the posts I made this week.

"Have you started posting on TikTok with those videos?" Michael asks. "I managed to get onto BookTok, and they go crazy for some hot hockey players."

"I haven't, but I'll have to see what I can do to fix that," I tell him. "What's new with the two of you this week?"

"I was invited to speak at a conference next month in Hawaii," Matteo says.

"That's amazing. Are you tagging along?" I ask Michael.

"Do you expect anything else from me? I can't let my hot husband go lay out on a beach without me." He smirks as he looks Matteo up and down like he's ready to pounce on him.

"None of that, now, you know I'm not down for being the third wheel, even if you both are hot." I scrunch up my nose at him, which just grants me an eye roll.

"When do you have to start traveling with the team?" Matteo asks.

"The first road trip is next week. It's just a pre-season

game but should be exciting and will be a taste of what's to come for the season. I've never traveled full-time with a team, so I'm sure it will be an adjustment."

"You'll do great, and maybe being in a hotel will make it easier to fall for one of the hot hockey boys," Michael teases.

I just chuckle and shake my head. He's stuck on this idea that I'll end up with one of the guys. I just think he's love drunk from his own happy relationship.

I enjoy the rest of my evening with my best friends. It's always a good time when we're together. By the time I make it home, I'm exhausted. Today was a long one at work. I spent hours upon hours editing images and footage, as well as finishing going through all the forms the players turned in. I followed or, at least, requested to follow all of them from the team's accounts as well as my own, since I will sometimes post from my own. I also made files on each player that are easy for me to access on the go so I know who needs footage sent to PR managers or whomever controls their posting.

I wash my face and brush my teeth before changing into some pjs. Once tucked into bed, I check some of my notifications and notice that I've had a few follow requests accepted, as well as being followed back by them. I click on the first, Damien Thompson's, and scroll through his pictures. He's always so quiet when I see him, kind of broody, and I'm intrigued by what I'll find on his private account. He's a typical guy, posts a few pictures, if that, each year. I quickly realize that wasn't always the case. He used to post all the time, mostly pictures of a woman, one I can only assume was his wife based on the images of them together and the captions. I scroll all the way back to his oldest image and flip through every single post. The way this man looked at her is the way every woman dreams of being looked at by the love of her life.

I'm in tears when I reach the end. I learned by some posts that his wife, Kelly, was killed in a car accident. His posts really slowed at that point in his life, although he's never missed a post on her birthday or their anniversary. You can feel in his posts just how much he misses his wife. I can't even imagine what it must be like for him.

I glance at the time and realize that I've spent almost two hours poring over this man's account. I turn my phone screen off and set it down on my nightstand. I'm not tired after scrolling for so long and learning more about the mysterious man, so I pull out my kindle and read until I drift off to sleep.

Today is the first road trip, and I'm so excited. I get to the airport thirty minutes before the team was instructed to arrive. I've never flown on a private charter, so this is all new to me. I'm greeted by an employee who shows me out onto the tarmac and directly onto the jet. They take my roller bag, and I watch as they load it directly on. I head up the staircase that has been rolled up to the open door of the jet.

"Welcome aboard." I'm greeted by a cheery-looking flight attendant. "I'm Mandy," she says.

"Nice to meet you. I'm Trinity. I'm the team's social media manager," I tell her, in case she needs to know who I am.

"Nice to meet you. You can select any seat within the first ten rows. It's open seating, for the most part. The guys have from row twelve and back."

"Thank you," I tell her as I find a seat. I pull out my main camera, along with two lens options. "Is it okay if I get off to take some arrival footage?" I ask.

"Of course. Did you want anything to drink or snack on before everyone starts to arrive?"

"I'm good for now but thank you."

"No problem. If that changes, just let me know. I also have a light lunch we'll be serving once in the air," she tells me.

"I'm not sure I'll get used to this," I tell her.

"Give it a few weeks and you'll be a pro at it. This is a fantastic team to work with. I've been with them since the first season, and they've been nothing but great to me the entire time."

"That's wonderful to hear. I've had the same experience so far in the few weeks I've been with them," I tell her. "What do you do once the team has arrived in their destination?" It might be nice to have another woman who looks to be my age on the road with me.

"Depending on how long we're in each city, I explore. It is also my job to work with all the vendors to keep the flight stocked with all the necessities, make up the menu and work with the chefs to make sure what we want is available. That reminds me, if you have any dietary restrictions, whether they are just preferences, or allergies, let me know and we can work around them. But otherwise, I attend some of the games, or sometimes I take the time to relax in my hotel room. I'm taking some college classes to finish up my degree, so I take advantage of the quiet when I have it."

"Sounds like an interesting job, if you're up for it, maybe we can grab coffee in our downtime," I suggest.

"I'd love that. I admit, I sometimes feel like an outcast since I'm one of the only women who travels with the team on a regular basis, so it will be nice to have you around."

"I was wondering how many of us there were, especially ones that travel. I know the front office is filled with women, but they don't travel."

"Exactly. Once we're in the air, we can exchange phone numbers," Mandy says. "But get on out there, it looks like some guys are on their way out." She points over my shoulder toward the private airport building. I turn around quickly and, sure enough, I see some of the guys headed this way. I step out of the plane but stand on the small landing at the top of the stairs and snap a handful of images before I descend the steps and switch over to my phone, where I capture a short video clip.

"Morning, ma'am," one of the guys greets me. I don't feel old enough to be greeted so formally, and it leaves me speechless. He's halfway up the stairs before I think of a comeback, but by that time, some more guys are headed my way.

I stay down on the tarmac, switching between snapping pictures and taking video. I've already decided that I need to get a small tripod that I can set up with a video camera to just record for the entire time. I can edit the footage down to smaller clips that will be used for social media posts and such while I'm on board. By having that, it will allow me to just focus on the images I take and not have to juggle multiple devices.

"Did you get everyone?" Mandy asks once I've climbed back up the stairs.

"Yes, I think I've got some good footage to work with. There's Wi-Fi on board, correct?"

"Absolutely. There should be a little card in the pocket of your seat that has instructions on how to connect. I reboot it before every flight, just to make sure everything is working properly, so you should be good to go once connected."

"Perfect! Can I bother you for a bottle of water when you have a moment?"

"Of course, let me grab you one," Mandy says as she ducks into her area and returns with an ice-cold bottle of water.

"Thanks," I tell her before I turn to head back to my seat. I get settled, placing my bag in the seat next to me so I have it close for after we take off. I want to start editing the footage and images I took so I can hopefully post a few before we even make it to Seattle.

CHAPTER 5
DAMIEN

I WALK DOWN THE BLOCK TO STARBUCKS. I SWEAR THERE IS ONE on every corner in this city. I pull open the door and notice that the person at the end of the line of six people is none other than Trinity. I observe her standing there as she looks down at her phone screen. She's scrolling through something —what? I have no idea, since I'm not that close to her. The line shuffles forward, so I take my place behind her.

I stay quiet. It's my normal modus operandi. I like to observe. You can learn a lot about someone by just watching them. Trinity is so engrossed in her phone, she never turns around and notices me during the time it takes us to move ahead.

I stay the appropriate distance behind her while she orders. Close enough I can hear her and I'm a little surprised she's not one to have some crazy ridiculous coffee order.

"I'm sorry, ma'am, but your card declined, would you like to try it again?"

"It did?"

"Yes, sorry. Our machine does that occasionally, just try again," the girl behind the counter says. I watch as Trinity taps her card, only for the machine to beep once again.

"Shit," I hear Trinity curse. "I'm sorry, I only have one card with me, I need to call my bank and find out what is wrong. Can you cancel my order?"

"No problem, sorry about that," the girl tells her, and she steps away. "Welcome, what can I get you today, sir?" the girl asks me as I step forward.

"I'd like to buy that lady her order, plus I'll take a Grande nitro brew with sweet cream on top."

"That's very kind of you, anything else?"

"That's all, thank you." I pull up the app on my phone and scan it to pay for the order, then step down toward the pickup counter. I keep an eye on Trinity. She's sitting down at a small table in the corner, her phone pressed to her ear as she talks to someone. I can see the look of worry on her face as she speaks.

It takes a few minutes before my name is called and the two drinks are ready. I grab both, and slowly walk toward the table she's sitting at. She puts the phone down but is cradling her face in her open palms.

I'm starting to feel a little out of place, not sure what to do now that I'm standing next to her with her drink, while something is obviously wrong.

I clear my throat, doing my best to get her attention. Her head pops up, and I can now see that she's been crying.

"Oh, hi," she says, wiping her face.

"Everything okay?" I ask.

"Not really," she says.

"Did you get ahold of your bank?" I nod toward the cell phone on the table.

"Um, yes," she says, questioning how I knew she was calling her bank.

"I was behind you in line. Here this is for you, I paid for it after you walked away from the register."

"Oh, wow. Thank you," she stammers.

"You're welcome. So, everything okay with the bank?" I ask.

"If some asshole stealing my card number and using it to go on a shopping spree is okay, then yes. I'm peachy."

"Oh shit, are they going to credit it back to you?"

"The fraud department is supposed to call me back shortly. The girl I spoke with cut off my card number; not that it matters any since they spent every last dime I had in my account. But she said once the fraud department got ahold of me and could go over all the charges and determine which transactions are fraud and which ones are legit, they can start the process of returning my money. I also have to get a new card, which sucks since it was the only one I brought with me."

"If you need anything the rest of the trip, let me know, I can help you out," I find myself offering. Why? I have no fucking idea. I have this immediate desire to protect this woman. Where that desire came from, I don't fucking know. If I really start to think about it, I get a little freaked out. I haven't felt like that since Kelly was alive.

"That's super sweet of you, but I'll be okay."

"The offer stands," I reiterate.

"Thanks." She takes a sip of the drink I set down for her. "And thanks for this. I could really use the caffeine, especially after that call."

"Understandable." I take a sip of my own coffee. The jolt of caffeine hitting my veins and getting me ready to hit the ice in a little while. "Are you heading back to the hotel?"

"Yes, I didn't really plan to stick around here, but then, the card issue," she explains.

"I'm headed that way, if you're ready." I find myself inviting her to walk with me.

I wait as she gathers her things and slides from the chair. She's petite, only reaching my shoulder at her full height. I know I'm tall at six foot five, but she's fucking tiny compared to my large body.

We head outside, and walk a few hundred feet, side-by-side, in complete silence.

"I stalked your Instagram page," she blurts.

I quirk a brow. "Find anything interesting?" I ask.

"I'm sorry about your wife. She was beautiful."

"Thank you, and she was. The best woman I've ever known," I tell her.

"Thanks for accepting my request, by the way."

"Figured it was only fair and will make your job easier. I used to have my page set to public, but after Kelly died, I couldn't deal with all the comments from everyone. They were overwhelming."

"I can only imagine," she says. "Have you thought of making a second page? One where you only post about hockey and can connect with your fans?"

"Not really. I've become somewhat of a recluse since she died. Ask any of the guys and they'll tell you just how often I go out with them. You can probably count the times on one hand. I almost gave up on my career after she died, but my father-in-law reminded me that she'd want me to continue chasing my dream and to live my life to the fullest."

"And are you doing that? Chasing your dream and living life to the fullest?" she asks.

I chuckle. If she only knew. "Chasing my dream, yes. Living life to its fullest, probably not," I admit.

"What's holding you back?"

"I don't really know," I admit.

We arrive at the hotel's main entrance, and I step ahead of Trinity so I can pull open the door for her to walk through. "Thank you," she says as she steps past me. The lightness of her perfume hits my senses and I want to breathe it deep into my lungs.

"Are you going with the team to morning skate?"

"I am, I was just trying to get coffee, first. But you know how that turned out." She chuckles at the situation.

"Are you enjoying your new job so far?" I ask.

"Absolutely. It is exactly what I dreamed it would be. Everyone has been so welcoming and great to work with. I don't even mind the smell that comes off the ice with you guys after practice." She laughs as she pinches her nose as if to block the smell.

I can't help but laugh at that. "Hockey players have a stench of their own, I'll give you that one."

"I thought the baseball players were bad, but they've got nothing on you guys."

I find my hackles going up at the thought of her hanging out in the dugout with a baseball team. How many of those guys have hit on her constantly?

"How long have you been working as a photographer?" I ask instead.

"I've been taking pictures since I was a teenager. Professionally, for the past four years. I did a season with a minor league baseball team, and then the last few years I've worked with the same minor team, as well as their major league affiliate. I was an independent contractor, so I didn't work every game like I will with the Shockwaves."

"Have you always been a hockey fan?"

She shakes her head no. "I've watched a few games here and there, but I have no idea what the rules are or what's going on, other than the goal is to get the little black puck into the net."

"Into the goal, but yes, that's the basics." I chuckle at her simple knowledge of the game. "If you ever have a game-specific question, I'd be happy to explain it to you."

"Thanks," she says as we both step onto the elevator. "Fifth floor, please," she says as I go to hit the button for the same floor.

"They stuck you on the same floor as the players, interesting," I state.

"Do they not normally put everyone on the same floor?"

"Coaching staff likes to have a little barrier between players. I think, so it doesn't feel so much like we're being watched. We aren't teenagers that need chaperones while on the road."

"That makes sense. Do you have to share rooms with each other?"

"Younger guys do sometimes, but once you're a veteran, we get our own rooms."

"Do guys' families ever travel with them on road trips?" she asks.

"Sometimes, but they aren't allowed to travel with us on the team jet or stay in our rooms. They can stay at the same hotel, but we aren't supposed to have anyone stay in our rooms."

"I suppose they want you guys to not have distractions keeping you up at night, especially on the road for games."

"Exactly. Some guys push the rules, hooking up with women they meet after games, but for the most part, guys follow the rules." I notice she scrunches up her nose at the thought of guys hooking up with random chicks. The elevator doors slide open and I wait for Trinity to step off before I follow her. We stand in the elevator lobby, finishing our conversation.

"Do they do that often? Hooking up with—what was the term I was reading, puck bunnies?"

I chuckle at her unease at the idea. "It just depends on the guy. I won't lie, I've had a good chunk of teammates over the years that had a different hookup in each city we visited. But that definitely isn't every guy, and probably less than your mind is calculating it to be. I can't think of any guys on this roster that I've noticed are that way. Most of the guys are all settled down or on their way to being settled down."

"And you, where do you fall in that group?"

"There hasn't been anyone serious since Kelly," I tell her honestly. Her eyes widen at my admission.

"Wow, she must have been one hell of a woman."

"She was. The best, and I know how lucky I was to call her mine."

Trinity's phone rings, and she looks down at it. "It's the bank, I need to take this. Thanks for the coffee." She holds up the cup as she brings the phone to her ear and takes off down the hall. I follow slowly, I don't want her to think I'm eaves-dropping as we both walk to our rooms, which just so happen to be next to one another. She quickly disappears inside her door, so I do the same, needing to get my shit together and ready to get on the bus in a little while for morning skate.

CHAPTER 6
TRINITY

"Hello," I answer the call.

"Hi, is this Miss Black?"

"Yes, this is her," I answer the man on the phone.

"Hello, Ms. Black; this is Phil from Community Bank's fraud department. I'm calling to follow up with you regarding the claim you opened. Is this a good time to go over everything with you?" he asks.

"Yes," I tell him as I enter my room. I head straight for the desk and pull out a notebook from my backpack, flipping it open to a blank page. After verifying my identity, he jumps right into going charge by charge from the last few days to determine just how many are fraudulent and what ones are valid from me. After everything is said and done, we've come up with ten charges that total more than six-thousand dollars. My stomach sinks when he advises that the process to return the money can sometimes take a few days but assures me they will waive any fees that I'm assessing for overdrawn fees and will get my money returned to me as soon as possible. My new card has already been ordered, so I'll hopefully have that within a day or two.

"I'm sorry that you were a victim like this, it happens to so many people every day. If you don't already, I suggest using things like Apple Pay or similar, when possible. By not inserting your card into a reader, it takes away the chance of the programmed details from being skimmed and reproduced. It also creates a one-time use card number the merchant received that can't be used more than the one time."

"I didn't know that, but thanks for the advice. I'll start doing that, when possible."

"Anytime. If you see anything else suspicious pop up on your account in the next few days, you can call back and give your case number and we can add it to it your case."

"I'll probably be checking the app multiple times a day to make sure nothing else pops in."

"Sounds good. I don't think anything else should be able to, since we shut down the card already, but it has happened on occasion if a merchant was slow to close out their card machine. However, I don't think that will happen in your case since all the charges were made online and not with a physical card."

I get off the phone with my bank and am relieved to have that over with. It sucks that it happened, but I'm relieved that they are working so quickly to get things fixed.

I open my bag and dig around to see if I have my larger wallet that has my back-up credit card. I'm relieved when I find it. Now I can at least buy myself a damn cup of coffee if need to before we return home.

I BOARD THE MOTOR COACH THAT WILL TAKE US TO THE RINK FOR morning skate and realize only the coaching staff is on board. "Morning," I greet as I walk past them at the front, taking a seat just a few rows back.

"Morning, Trinity, how are things going for you?" Coach asks.

"It's going great, everyone has been cooperative, so far," I tell him.

"Good to hear. Let me know if they give you any shit and I'll put an end to it."

"Thanks," I tell him before he turns back to the other coaches he was having a conversation with. I'm sure they go over practice plans, as well as game plans for later tonight.

I pop in my earbuds and turn on a podcast I enjoy listening to. I open up Instagram and get a new image that I edited last night up on the team's page, as well as post a few clips in stories. With those posted, I scan through some of the comments, replying back on a few of them.

I feel him before my eyes land on the large body that takes up the space next to me. I glance over at Damien, flashing him a shy smile before I pop my earbud out of my right ear.

"Get everything taken care of with your bank?" he asks.

"Yes, they are working on it, and I should have all my money back within a couple of days, as well as a new debit card."

"Good to hear."

"And I found my larger wallet with my back-up credit card, so I can buy my own coffee tomorrow morning," I tell him.

"I didn't mind," he says. I don't know what to make of this man. He's got that large and in charge vibe going, but also is known to be the quiet and broody type. However, my interactions with him have shown me something very different. "What are you working on?" he asks, nodding his head toward my phone.

"Just a few posts for the fans to see how pre-season camp is going," I tell him and then show him the video I edited.

"You did all of this?" he asks.

"I did," I confirm.

"Damn, you are talented," he praises me and I can't help but smile at his words.

"Thanks. It's hardly work when you love what you do."

"Isn't that the truth."

We fall into a comfortable silence as the bus fills up and we start moving. The drive to the arena isn't that long, maybe fifteen minutes, at most. I gather my things and exit the bus, but pull my camera out and step aside so that I can get the guys coming off and entering the rink. I make a mental note to stick around and get some footage of the equipment guys after morning skate and before the game. The feedback from my behind-the-scenes posts have been getting a ton of positive responses, and they always ask for more.

I take a seat in the top of the bowl; this gives me a view of the entire ice from above the glass. I get some shots of the team all huddled around the coaches as they give out their orders before the start. It's mesmerizing to watch the group all take off, splitting into two lines each one taking half the ice. They effortlessly move from skating laps to shooting drills. Some of the guys stay around center ice, stretching out their legs before popping up and joining one of the groups.

They move about like the professionals they are. Switching from one drill to the next, without any instructions from the coaches. I snap a few pictures as guys stop to talk with a trainer or equipment manager. One of the players comes off the ice and onto the bench, and I jump up to capture the footage. I watch as the equipment manager pops the skate blade right out of the holder and pops new ones in. I had no idea that was even possible, so I'm sure people will love seeing that. Once he's back on the ice, I re-watch the short video clip, edit it quickly on my phone, and get it uploaded to all our social media platforms.

At the advice of Matteo and Michael, I've been checking out the hype on TikTok with hockey teams. They weren't kidding when they said people are going crazy over teams. I love the videos where they ask all the players a specific question, so I've set up a little Q&A station for all of them to walk by after they get off the ice.

I see Blake, one of the goalies, headed my way, so I hold out the mini microphone to him. He's got a big ol' smile on his face as he reads the question I've written out in large font across my notebook. "What's your guilty pleasure?"

"Damn, girl, you go right for it," he teases as he thinks over the question. A few of the other guys come up behind him, all stopping to read what I've written down. "I'd have to go with Caramellos. They are the perfect mixture of chocolate and caramel."

"Guilty pleasure, huh?" Ryker says. "I'll keep it clean and say cookies." He winks at the camera before sauntering off into the locker room.

I can't help but chuckle at their double entendre answers.

"Mine's coffee," Damien answers, only, he winks at *me*, not the camera. Was he just flirting with me? I don't have time to ponder that as the rest of the guys are all coming in behind him, answering the question so fast, I can't even keep up. Good thing I've got this all on camera and can watch it back when I edit it later.

Once everyone is back in the locker room, I go in search of the equipment guys to find out their schedule.

"Is it okay if I shadow you guys today?" I ask Ian, the head equipment manager.

"Sure can; do you want us to explain what we're doing as we do it or do you want to just capture footage?"

"If you can explain what you're doing and why you do it, that'd be awesome."

"No problem," he says.

"A quick rundown is we wait until the guys are done in the locker room, then we head in there and collect everything. They leave all their gear in their locker spots but have bins to toss everything that needs washing. Arenas all have laundry facilities for us to use, as well as repair areas. It is amazing how many times we have to fix broken equipment on a daily basis."

"Wow, I didn't think about those aspects."

"We are jacks of all trades, when you think of it." He chuckles. "Once the guys clear out, we head in and start prepping for the game. All equipment gets a once over for any damage that needs tending to. Skate blades are checked and swapped out for new ones, if needed. The final step is setting out their game uniforms. Every station gets set up exactly the same. While two of us are working on the locker room, the other is getting laundry going and sharpening blades. We keep two to three extra sets of blades for each player, sharpened and ready to go in case we need to swap out during a game. We can do that in a matter of a few minutes, usually quick enough that a player won't even miss a shift."

"That's amazing."

"Once the locker room is reset, we make sure water bottles, and their sports drinks of choice, are prepped. Then comes the fun things, like setting up the warmup pucks on the ledge of the boards."

"Do you get a break at all or downtime before the team comes back to the rink?" I ask.

"We try. The bus brings the guys back around four, so if it's close to that time, then we just hang out here all day."

"And how late after a game?" I ask, realizing just how much these guys do for the team.

"We're usually some of the last out, and first ones in. After the game tonight, we'll completely pack everything up and get it loaded onto a box truck that will take it back to the plane. We travel with these large crates that never get fully unpacked, except for the items that we actually use, so some of what we bring, like all the extra skate blades, extra jerseys, equipment, etc., all stays packed. Packing the player bags isn't that hard, since we have a well-oiled system and, like the stalls, the bags are all packed the same way so everything fits just how we want it to."

"That makes perfect sense."

I've gotten so engrossed in our conversation, I didn't even realize the guys have been filing out of the locker room. "Looks like we've got the 'all clear' and can head in and get started," Ian tells me.

I follow him in and the pungent smell of sweat hits me face first. "Holy crap." I gag.

Ian laughs at my disgusted face. "You get used to it."

"How?" I breathe through my mouth and cover it with the collar of my shirt.

"Years and years of working in a hockey locker room, not much fazes me anymore."

"You are a saint," I tell him as I start to slowly spin in a circle, capturing footage of the entire room.

"Since this is a pre-season game, we have more guys than we will during the regular season. That makes it a little more crowded in here than normal," Ian explains as he starts at the end of the row. Noah, one of the other equipment managers, joins us and starts on the other end, working toward Ian. They are incredibly fast, checking over the equipment just like Ian said they would and rearranging it just how they want it to be.

It doesn't take them more than forty-five minutes to completely revamp the room, including freshening up the air so the stench of sweaty man isn't the only thing in here.

We move on to the rest of their duties and have everything wrapped up with two hours to spare before the guys will return, so we decided to grab an Uber and head back to the hotel for an afternoon break.

CHAPTER 7
DAMIEN

I take the same seat on the bus as I was in on the ride over to the rink. However, this time, I don't have the beautiful brunette sitting next to me. I wait impatiently as the rest of my teammates all get on board, along with the coaching staff, but still, no Trinity.

"Hey, Coach, aren't we forgetting someone, I don't see Trinity on the bus?" I holler up to him as the bus driver starts to pull away from the curb.

"No, Trinity stayed back with the equipment guys. Wanted some footage on how they operate on away game days."

I nod in understanding, all the while, grinding my molars at the thought that she's hanging out with other guys. As the thoughts run through my head, I shake them right out. What in the hell is coming over me right now when it comes to her?

I slip my earbuds in and turn on some music. Maybe if I have something else to focus on, I won't focus on Trinity.

As soon as we reach the hotel, I grab some lunch from the ballroom they have set up for the team. I like to eat a larger lunch, then a smaller snack before the game.

"You ready for tonight?" Aiden asks as we take a seat at the same table.

"If Coach puts me in, I'll be ready," I tell him. Not all the veterans play during the pre-season. Our spots are protected and guaranteed. The younger guys, not so much. Coach hasn't told us the lines yet for tonight, that information usually comes once we arrive at the arena and have our pre-game meeting. "What about you, feeling well rested? The baby keeping you up a lot lately?"

"I'm good, and no, he's a great sleeper. Has slept all through the night for a while now. What's up with you chatting it up with the photographer?" he asks as Ryker, Tristan, and Blake all join our table.

"Just being friendly. She had a mishap at the coffee shop this morning and I was there to step in and help, that's all. She's also extremely talented with what she's posting. Have you seen any of the videos?" I ask the guys.

"Tori sent me the link to one, told me I needed to watch it," Aiden says. "It was good, I can see why they hired her."

"I can't wait to see what she does from today's question of the day she filmed," Ryker admits.

"Yeah, I think some of the guys were quite brazen," Blake adds.

"Better keep the boys in line, Cap. Don't want any sexual harassment claims against someone on the team." I say.

"I'll say something to make sure everyone keeps it appropriate," Ryker says. "Just kind of interesting how much of an interest you, of all people, are taking in her," he adds.

I don't say anything, because as much as I don't want to admit it, he's one hundred percent correct.

"Cat got your tongue?" Tristan snickers. "Or is the notoriously broody and introverted Damien actually coming out of his cave?"

"Fuck off," I tell him, however, there isn't much behind my words. The smirk on his face, hell, all the guys' faces at the table say that they have noticed the change in my demeanor. I can't say I don't like it, because I do. I just don't know what to do about that.

I TOSS AND TURN, NOT GETTING A WINK OF SLEEP DURING MY nap. This isn't normal. I'm usually able to fall asleep within minutes and get a good siesta in before it's time to get up and ready for the bus.

I toss off the covers, my room is sweltering today, which probably isn't helping much with my sleeping. A glance at the clock tells me that I'm only twenty minutes from my alarm going off, so it is pointless to try and continue to fall asleep. I get up and adjust the thermostat down, waiting to move until I hear the air conditioner kick on.

I lay back down but grab my phone. My thumb hovers over the Instagram app, hesitating if I should open it to check out Trinity's work.

I set my phone back down, closing my eyes and thinking about Kelly. "*I miss you, Honey. I need you to tell me what to do. Why am I so drawn to this woman? Did you send her to me?*" I've had many moments like this one where I just want to talk to my wife. Ask her all the hard questions, or better yet, trade places with her. I still don't know how I've managed to continue living without her for so long. She's been gone longer than I had her in my life, and that's not something I like to think about.

Like always, I never get an answer to my questions. Not that I expect one, but some days it would be nice.

My alarm goes off, so I drag myself out of bed and to the shower. I take a cold one, hoping the biting coldness of the water will help pull me from my funk. It cools my skin down but does nothing to cool the burning I have inside my gut that's churning.

I close my eyes as I wash the soap from my hair. As soon as my eyes close, I see Trinity. Her smiley face. Her beautiful curves. My eyes fly open, soap be damned as I shake those thoughts from my mind. I have no right to think of her like that.

I continue to rinse the remaining soap out, then move on to washing my body. When I reach my groin, my cock swells and more thoughts of Trinity flood my mind. I imagine pinning her against the shower wall. I'd trail kisses all over her throat as I slammed into her until we were both coming apart. My hand wraps around my swollen girth, giving in to my need to come.

I let my mind continue to wander and wonder what she'd look like sprawled out over my bed. What her pussy would taste like if I was to slide my tongue along the seam of her most intimate parts. What it would be like to hear my name fall from her lips as I wrapped mine around her clit and sucked until she came against my mouth.

My hand moves faster and faster as I feel my release building. My balls feel heavy as they fill, so I cup them with my other hand, giving them a little tug as I shuttle my palm faster and faster up and down my length. The tingling at the base of my spine quickly moves down, just as my balls tighten up and my orgasm comes barreling out of me and all over the shower wall. I collapse against the tile, my exhaustion hitting me hard as I gulp in air. *Fuck, I need to get laid.*

Once I've caught my breath and my heart rate is back to normal, I do my best to clean the wall off before I finish washing up and get out of the shower. Once dried off, I wrap my towel around my waist while I stand at the bathroom sink, brush my teeth and comb my hair before it's time to pull on the suit I brought for today's game.

With as many years in the league as I have, I've accumulated a number of suits. As the years went by, those suits became nicer and more expensive. I've learned what a good tailor can do for a guy of my stature.

I finish buttoning the cuffs on my shirt, then make sure the ends are tucked nicely into my slacks. I return to the bathroom and spritz on some cologne. One last look at my hair, and I'm satisfied with how I look. I snag my suit coat off the bed, tuck my wallet into my back pocket and slip my phone into my front one.

I check my watch and the bus should be outside and ready for us to board, so I head for the door. I step out of my room, just as the door next to mine opens. Trinity fills her doorway, and I can't help but be mesmerized by her presence. If I was a blushing man, I might be embarrassed by the thoughts I had of her while I was in the shower, but thankfully, I'm not.

"Hi," she says, and if I wasn't mistaken, it was a little breathy.

"Hi," I say, my voice a little gruff.

"Did you have a good nap?" she asks.

"Couldn't fall asleep, not sure why," I tell her honestly.

"Oh, does that happen often?"

Only when I can't get a certain brunette off my mind. "No, I think my room was just too hot," I tell her instead.

"Mine was quite warm when I got back. Housekeeping must have turned them up when they were in this morning," she suggests.

"Maybe," I reply. "How was hanging out with Ian's crew?"

"Are you keeping track of me?" She smiles up at me.

"We were worried the bus was leaving without you, so Coach let us know where you were," I tell her as we make our way to the elevator.

"Aww, how sweet. The hockey players were all worried about the photographer," she coos.

I just grunt in response, hoping that my cover isn't blown that *I* was the only hockey player that was worried.

"Back to your question, I learned a lot and had a good time. Ian and Noah were great and explained so much about their jobs. I can't wait to edit the video footage I took."

"That's good," I say as I hold out an arm to hold the elevator door open and allow Trinity to get on first. As I walk behind her, a few of the other guys approach, so I hold the door for them, as well.

We're all silent on the short ride down to the lobby. The guys who rode down with us are guys fighting for a spot on the roster. Both are good players, but I don't know if they'll secure permanent spots or if they'll be sent back down to the AHL and called up, as needed, when we have guys out with injuries.

We arrive at the arena and I head straight for the changing room. I strip from my suit, changing into some athletic shorts and a t-shirt, as do all the other guys. Some of us hit the warmup bikes, while others start sprints down the long hallways. We eventually break into groups, kicking around a soccer ball as we all get loosened up.

"Anyone need to be stretched?" one of the trainers calls out as he steps out of his treatment room.

"I do," Blake calls out and leaves our group. As a goalie, he's required to be flexible, and that comes from hours of stretching and learning to flex his body in different ways.

"Locker room in ten," Coach calls out after we've been warming up for a good hour.

I stop at the snack table that is set up and grab a protein bar and bottle of water. I need to keep hydrated and refuel my body. The trainers will start making protein shakes specific to our needs while Coach goes over the game plan for tonight.

"Tristan and Damien, you're in the box tonight," Coach says, turning to Tristan and me. We both knew this was a huge possibility so we both nod our agreement with him.

Coach finishes up his line-up plans, along with what he's looking for tonight from the guys that will be on the ice.

"That's all from me, get some food, and I'll see you out on the ice when it's time," he says before heading out of the room. The guys start milling around. The training staff starts coming in with the protein shakes. I take mine and down it. Even though I'm not playing tonight, I can still use the extra nutrition.

CHAPTER 8
TRINITY

"ARE YOU TAKING PICTURES ALL GAME?" DAMIEN ASKS AS I stand near the glass. I make a double take as I'm not expecting to see him behind me, especially dressed in his suit again.

"Probably, but why aren't you out on the ice?" I ask, slightly worried that something is wrong. He doesn't look in distress, but what do I know about this guy?

"I'm not in the lineup tonight. During pre-season, not all the veteran players play every game. Some of us have to sit so the guys fighting for those last few roster spots can play and duke it out."

"Makes sense," I murmur as I put the lens of my camera back into the little cutout they have in the Plexiglas for the media. I snap a few pictures of Blake as he catches the puck in his glove like the expert goalie he is.

"So, are you staying down here all game?" Damien asks.

"I'm not sure where else I'd go. I don't think Coach wants me on the bench."

"You can come up to the visitors' press box with Tristan and me."

"I can?" I turn toward him, giving him my attention.

"I don't see why not. Did you get a team credentials pass?"

"Yeah," I tell him as I hold up the pass that has my photo, name, and what my title is with the team. It also says full access, since I'm granted access to the team at all times.

"Then you are allowed to be in the press box. It isn't anything fancy, but it can be a cool view of the game," he says. "I can also explain what is going on, answer any questions you might have about the game."

"Then show me the way," I tell him, a little giddy that I'll get to experience the game from a different vantage point, and to get his expert teaching about the game.

The press box is up high, almost all the way to the rafters, it seems. It is definitely a different view of the ice from up here, but nothing my zoom lens can't handle. I take a seat in one of the plush chairs and set up my long-range lens. I snap a few pictures of the team in warmups before they all head off the ice before the start of the game.

Tristan and Damien both join me, taking the seats on either side of me. My mind momentarily dips into the gutter, thinking how so many puck bunnies would think they'd died and gone to heaven to be flanked by these two men and all the dirty things they could do to me. I shake those thoughts right out of my mind. I can't be thinking like that while I'm working, not to mention the fact that Tristan is a married man.

"Is this guy giving you any shit?" Tristan asks, nodding his head in Damien's direction.

I give him a confused look, "Um, no," I tell him. "The opposite, actually. He's been very welcoming and helpful," I tell him.

"Interesting." Tristan smiles wide. "I think it took a month or so after we met to get more than a grunt out of him." He chuckles. "He was a hard one to crack, still isn't much of a talker some days."

"I'm right here, asshole." Damien laughs from my other side.

"I think he's smitten with you," Tristan says, ignoring Damien. "I have never seen him so chatty with someone in the few years I've known him now."

I don't really know what to do with that information. It isn't like I've sought him out when I'm at work. The more that I think about it, he's the one that is always popping up where I'm at.

"There's nothing wrong with being friendly," Damien grumbles.

I turn my attention back to him, giving him a friendly smile. "And I appreciate it. I wasn't sure what I'd be walking into with a group of professional athletes. Sometimes guys can be a bit full of themselves and think that everyone else should bow down to their greatness. I haven't experienced that at all with anyone on this team."

"You've experienced it with other athletes?" Tristan asks.

"Oh yeah. The first season I worked with a pro baseball team. There were a couple guys on the roster who thought they were God's gift to mankind and women. They definitely thought I would sleep with them just because of who they were."

"What pricks," Damien says.

"They didn't like the fact I turned them down, especially when I made sure to do so in front of the coaching staff. I'm pretty sure the entire team got chewed out after that and were reminded of the fraternization policy. I was actually surprised they took everything so seriously."

"Professional organizations don't usually like sexual assault scandals. Just look at how badly the football team in DC has been raked through the media over the allegations that have come out from former female employees," Tristan says.

"While I don't think anyone here would act that way, we

don't have a no fraternization policy that I'm aware of," Damien says.

"Interesting, and now that you mention that, I don't remember one being outlined in my new hire paperwork."

The lights in the rink darken as the spotlights start roaming around the ice. The PA announcer comes over the speakers and gets the crowd cheering as we wait for the players to take the ice. The crowd boos as the refs skate out. I watch as they take a few laps around. Two of them check the nets, making sure none of the lacing is loose from the frame or that any holes are present that shouldn't be there. In the meantime, both teams come back out, the crowd cheering for the home team.

Only the starting line ups take to the ice, each team's players lining up along the blue line for the PA announcer to read off the names of the starters before the national anthem is sung.

Once the anthem is finished, the lights come back on and the guys on the ice skate around, taking their position as the ref stands at center ice with the puck. I focus in on center ice, snapping a few images so quickly I get the movement from the ref holding the puck up, to it dropping down to the ice. The game jumps to a quick start as the Shockwaves take control of the puck and head down the ice. The whistle blows just as they cross the blue line, but I have no idea why.

"Why'd they just stop the play?" I ask.

"We were offsides," Damien says. "The puck has to cross before any player on the offensive team fully crosses. You'll see guys straddle the line or drag a leg back to stay onsides, but they were clearly offsides with that entry."

"So, no penalty?" I ask.

Both guys chuckle. "No, just a neutral zone face-off. Coach might not be too happy about it, but it happens multiple times a game. If they hadn't called the offsides and we had gone on to score a goal, the opposing coach can challenge the goal as offside if he so chooses. The refs would then review the footage and if they determine the offsides was missed, the goal doesn't count. But if they are wrong, and the footage doesn't overturn the goal call, then they are assessed a two-minute bench minor for delay of game. So, coaches will usually only challenge calls if they are confident that it will be called in their favor," Damien explains.

"How do they know if they should challenge a call?" I ask.

"The video coaches are up in the box. They are watching closely for things like that. They will then talk to the coaches through their earpieces and tell them what they see. There are iPads down on the bench for them to review the footage, as well. A coach has to make the call quickly as they only have until the next face-off to alert the refs they want to challenge."

"Sounds intense," I murmur.

"They know what to look for, and most have a pretty good track record for only challenging ones that will go their way. The delay of game penalty has only been the rule for a handful of years. It used to be that the team would lose their only timeout of a game if they lost the challenge. I think the way they do it now is better," Tristan adds.

We continue to watch the game and the guys do a great job explaining everything that is happening and why calls are being made. About halfway through the first period, one of the rookies, Chase, gets an amazing break and skates the puck down and scores the first goal of the game. The home crowd groans about it, while the few Shockwaves fans all cheer for the goal.

By the middle of the second period, I've started to figure things out. I can tell as soon as the whistle blows that a play was offsides, and I'm slowly starting to understand icing. It wasn't anything like I thought it would be like, but when Tristan told me that the basics of the call is if the puck crosses two red lines without being touched by the defensive team, unless they are on the penalty kill, then it is icing. Knowing when and why they wave it off is a little more confusing, so they stopped trying to explain it to me.

The game gets really exciting in the third period when Seattle pulls their goalie to give the extra attacker and the game ends up tied up with only ninety seconds left. Everyone in the arena is on their feet, cheering loudly for their team to win.

At the end of regulation, it is still tied, so to overtime we go.

"Overtime is different for pre-season and regular season than it is in the playoffs. Pre-season and regular season, we have a minute break, then it is a five-minute sudden-death period, and we play three-on-three, plus goalies. If no one scores in those five minutes, then we go into a shootout until a winner prevails. In playoffs, we have a regular intermission and full twenty-minute periods, five-on-five, but still sudden death, and no shootouts," Damien tells me.

"Sounds intense. So, in playoffs, how many overtimes can there be?" I ask.

"As many as it takes for someone to score. There have been games that went into three and four overtimes."

My eyes about bug out of my head. "Isn't that like playing two complete games?" I ask.

"Yep," Tristan says. "The last team I played for had a game that went into triple overtime. It was exhausting. By the time a goal came, we all just about collapsed into the locker room."

"Did your team win?" I ask.

"Yes."

"Ask him who scored the game winner," Damien suggests.

My head swings from one guy to the other. "Who scored?" I ask and he's already smiling big.

"I did. Probably the most memorable goal of my professional career. Well, maybe besides my first one."

"I can only imagine what the celebration was like for that," I state.

"We celebrated, but we were also so exhausted by the time it happened that we just wanted to get out of there and back to the hotel and into bed. The game ended after midnight."

"Dang."

He starts to chuckle. "I remember watching some of the footage the next day and they showed fans trying to take naps on each other during the intermissions."

"That's a late game, but they sure got their money's worth."

"That they did," he agrees.

We watch as the teams battle it out on the ice. The Shock-waves have possession of the puck more than not, but the Seattle goalie is on fire and practically a brick wall against all the shots they send his way during overtime.

"Now comes the fun part," Damien says as the guys clear from the ice, except the goalies. The home team sends out one player and the refs set the puck at center ice. I snap a wide-angle picture, one that shows both goalies, and the player waiting behind the center ice line.

It's fun to watch as he's given the signal that he can proceed. He taps the puck, and it slides forward on his stick, he skates out wide toward the side boards, and our goalie adjusts, watching his every move. He cuts back in, bringing the puck along, before he shoots it right into Blake's chest plate.

"Fucking brick wall," Damien says about Blake's stop.

Coach sends Aiden out over the boards for our first shooter. He does the same as the other guy, waits for the signal from the refs, then is off. He takes the puck, but unlike the other guy, doesn't skate out so wide, he comes almost straight down the center. "Watch him closely," Tristan says. I do and as the goalie commits to falling forward as he attempts to poke check the puck off of Aiden's stick, he swipes it to the side and right around the goalie's leg and into the back of the net!

"We did it!" I cheer.

"Not so fast," Damien says as both guys chuckle. "Shootouts start with three shooters on each team and go to more, if needed."

"Oh." I sit back down and watch as the next guy comes out and, unfortunately, sneaks the puck past Blake.

Our second shooter isn't as lucky as Aiden, and Seattle's goalie plucks the puck right out of the air into his glove. Their third guy goes out and, unfortunately for him, the puck rolls off his stick just as he tries to shoot, and he completely misses his chance to put it on goal.

All comes down to our third guy, this time, the same rookie that scored the breakaway goal to open up scoring. I get my camera ready, filming this time, to hopefully capture the winning goal.

"Is he going to be cocky or smart." Damien states more than asks anyone.

"I think smart; he wants a spot on the roster," Tristan answers him as all three of us watch what he's going to do.

He picks up the puck from center ice, skates it a little wide. He keeps his head up and it appears he's watching the goalie. Trying to read what he's going to do. He skates up fairly close to the crease.

"He's trying to pull the goalie out," Damien says.

I hold my breath, hoping the guy knows what he's doing. The goalie flinches and that's all Chase needs to slip the puck between the legs and into the back of the net.

"Damn, he's good!" Tristan exclaims as the entire bench erupts in cheers and clears out onto the ice. They surround Chase as they celebrate his shootout win.

With the game over, we gather our things and head back down to ice level. The guys join the rest of the team in the locker room while I wait outside. Once media is given the greenlight to enter, I go inside to get some locker room footage. It might only be a pre-season game, but they are celebrating it. Chase is surrounded by media, all with recorders out as he answers their questions.

It amazes me how quickly the guys all get ready. Within an hour of the game ending, they are loading onto the bus and we're heading for the airport to fly back home tonight.

"Did you have fun tonight?" Mandy asks as she stops at my seat once we're in the air.

"I did. I sat up in the press box with Tristan and Damien. They explained the game to me, and I might actually understand most of what happened tonight," I tell her.

"How fun! They are great guys. Have you met Tristan's wife and daughter?" she asks.

"I haven't. I haven't met anyone not on the team or who works for the team."

"The families are all so nice," she says. "Tristan's wife, Kendra, owns a meal prep company and is an amazing chef. You should check out her website. I think the majority of her clients are from the team."

"Interesting. I'll have to check her out, then. My best friend and his husband have been trying out different companies, trying to find their favorite, so I'll have to see if they've heard of hers yet."

"I've suggested to the company who sources our meals that we look into hers, but so far, they haven't made that happen yet."

"Did you have a good time in Seattle?" I ask.

"I did. My sister lives here, so I got to see her and my niece. She's only nine months old and growing so fast. I love getting to see her when we come to town."

"Aww, I bet it was a great visit then."

"Can I get you anything? I have food if you're hungry, everything from some snack plates to full dinner plates."

"Something small would be great," I tell her.

"For small plates, I have a small salad, cheese plate with fruit and crackers, and a sushi plate. Do you have a preference?"

"Hmm, I'll go with the cheese plate."

"Good choice," she says before stepping away. I notice she checks in with a few other staff members before disappearing into her little nook area. A few minutes later, she returns with a tray that has the food plate along with silverware and a napkin. "Let me know if you need anything else."

Before I remove the cover on the cheese plate, I remember that I need to put my phone in airplane mode. I notice that I have a missed text from my dad, so I quickly read it and reply.

DAD

> Just checking in, hope the new job is going well. Call when you are free.

TRINITY

> Hey Dad, the job is AMAZING! I'm in Seattle right now, about to fly back. I'll try to call in the next day or so. Love and miss you and Mom. Tell her I said hi!

I turn on airplane mode and make a mental note to call my parents. It has been a little bit since I talked to them.

I dig in as Mandy continues back farther onto the plane, checking in with the players. When I look back, most of them are sleeping or appear to be deep in conversation with each other.

CHAPTER 9
DAMIEN

I slide out of bed, stretching as my muscles protest that they're no longer relaxing. It was after one this morning by the time I made it home and into bed. Thankfully, Coach gave us today off to recuperate after the away game yesterday. Even without playing, my body is ready for a break.

I grab a quick shower before making a plan for the day. I find myself wanting to get out of the house, which surprises even me.

> What are you doing today? Want to go grab breakfast somewhere?

TRISTAN

Who is this and what have you done to my line partner? Are you feeling okay? Running a fever? :laughing emoji: I'm up for a second breakfast. :smirking emoji:

> TMI dude. I didn't need to know that about you and Kendra.

Laughing emoji, devil emoji: Maybe we need to find you a nice woman. One who can put up with your broody ass. Then you will appreciate a good second breakfast joke.

I know all about second breakfast. I was enjoying them while you were still finding your dick.

Burn old man.

Are we eating or what? I'm starving.

So many jokes… Meet in twenty? Cozy Café?

Sounds like a plan. Is the family coming or just a table for two if I beat you there?

I can't leave my girls behind.

You are one pussy whipped man.

No better way to be.

I grab my keys and head for my sports car. The weather is perfect for a roof down kind of drive. The sun on my skin is warm already on this beautiful fall day.

I beat Tristan to the restaurant, which I figured I would, seeing as how I was basically ready to walk out of the door and I'm sure they had to get Olivia ready.

I'm seated at a corner table. One that can easily accommodate the adults and a highchair, which the hostess places at the end of the table.

I look over the menu while I wait for them to arrive, which takes them at least fifteen minutes to do so.

"So sorry we took forever," Kendra says as she approaches the table. "Little miss had a blow out just as I went to put her into the car seat. Required a full change for both of us." She leans over and gives me a side hug.

I shudder at the thought of such a little thing making such a huge mess.

"No problem," I assure her.

I watch as they get settled. Tristan takes the baby from her car seat and places her in the highchair, then places a sippy cup in her hands.

"We're just starting to try with the cup," Kendra tells me.

"Ah." I watch as Olivia struggles to get the spout into her mouth before dropping the cup to the ground. Tristan leans over and picks it up, wipes the top with a baby wipe that Kendra hands over, before he hands it back to Olivia. I can't help but smirk at them as this happens multiple times in a row before she finally gets it into her mouth and sucks on it long enough to get something out of it. I think it shocks her because of the face she makes when the liquid hits her mouth.

"Good morning, I'm Marjorie and I'll be your server this morning. Can I get you guys some drinks to start with?" she asks the table at large.

"I'll take a large iced coffee with a splash of cream," Kendra tells her.

"I'll start with a large glass of orange juice, and water," Tristan adds.

"And for you, sir?" she asks, turning her body my way.

"I'm good with water, thanks."

"All right, I'll give you a few minutes to look over the menu and be back to take your order."

"Thanks," Kendra says as Marjorie steps away.

"Hey, it's Trinity," Tristan says as he holds up a hand and waves at someone. I look over my shoulder and, sure enough, Trinity is standing at the hostess stand.

"Trinity, come join us," Tristan calls out. The restaurant isn't large, so she notices us immediately after he hollers at her. I can see the way her cheeks go red as if she's embarrassed by him calling her out.

"Hi," she says, approaching our table. "I don't want to interrupt your breakfast."

"You aren't interrupting anything," Kendra says to her. "I'm Kendra, you must be Trinity, I've heard about you from my husband, here." Kendra lays her head on Tristan's shoulder, and he kisses her head.

"Nice to meet you, and this must be your little girl I've heard about," Trinity gushes over Olivia.

"Aren't you just the sweetest," she says as she's dropped down closer to Olivia's level in the highchair and is allowing her to grip onto one of her fingers, which Olivia tries to pull into her mouth.

"Sorry about that, she's teething like crazy," Kendra says.

"No problem at all. She's super cute," Trinity tells her as she stands next to our table a little awkwardly. I slide over a little more, opening up a few more inches of space for her to join us.

"You're welcome to sit down and join us. We've only just ordered drinks," I tell her, just as our server returns with said drinks.

She looks between the three of us. I can tell she's contemplating the offer. The way she nibbles on her bottom lip has my cock twitching. I'd like to replace her teeth with my own.

"I guess it wouldn't hurt to join you guys," she finally says as she takes the open spot next to me. A light, sweet scent floats my way, and I find myself wanting to smell more of that. No idea if it's her shampoo, or perfume or what, but I'm quickly becoming addicted to it the more I'm around her.

We give the server our order; Trinity was able to quickly look over the menu while the three of us gave our orders.

"So, how are you liking working with the team?" Kendra asks Trinity once Marjorie steps away.

"I love it. I'm having so much fun. And thanks to these

two, I've learned a lot about the game after yesterday's game."

"That's great. It is nice to have someone as knowledgeable as the two of them to explain things."

"I was clueless but, just after watching one game, I feel like I have a good idea on what's going on now, and why certain calls are made."

"Do you only do sports photography?" Kendra asks.

"That's been my focus, but I've done some other things while I was building my portfolio."

"The WAGS are in charge of a charity auction in December, would you be willing to donate a photoshoot as an auction item?"

"Damn, you ladies are vultures." I chuckle.

"What did they get from you?" Trinity turns to ask me.

I grumble a little before answering, all while Kendra just cackles from her side of the table. "A date with me," I tell her sheepishly.

"A date with you." She quirks a brow, and I can see the wheels turning behind her eyes. They flash with some mischief as her lips turn up into a smile. "Now that is something I want to see happen. Can I be a fly on the wall at the actual date?" she asks.

"Maybe you should win the date," Kendra chimes in, her words coming out in a sing-song way.

Trinity shrugs her shoulders. "My guess is I'd quickly be outbid."

"Not if I gave you my credit card," I tell her, and the idea is planted into my head. If I have Trinity bid on me and win, then I don't have to worry about some crazy chick winning the date and thinking we're going to run off and fall in love together.

She squints at me as she processes my words. "And why would you do that?"

"Because then I know it isn't someone crazy who wins the

bid. We might not know one another all that well, but one thing I do know is you're not some crazy puck bunny."

"Are you sure about that?" she questions and attempts to hold back her laughter. My eyes flash across the table where both Tristan and Kendra are snickering at this conversation.

"Please do it, I'll pay big bucks to see you go crazy on his ass," Kendra says between fits of laughter.

Trinity just shrugs her shoulders at the idea. I have three months to convince her that she needs to bid until she's the winner. I didn't want to do this auction to begin with, but I do like this solution for going along with it.

THE WHISTLE BLOWS AGAIN, THIS TIME COACH MOTIONS FOR ALL of us to gather around so he can give further instructions. I grab a water bottle off the edge of the boards and take a few large gulps. My lungs burn for how hard he's been pushing us today.

"Good hustle out there, I want to see more of that as we go into this next drill," he says and continues to describe the play he wants us to run through.

Everyone disperses to their specific spots, and we jump right into what Coach has instructed us to do. We've only got one week left before the regular season opens up here at home, and I can't fucking wait for the season to officially get under way.

"Nice job out there, Damien," Coach calls out to me as I exit the ice.

I lift my head in his direction, he doesn't need any response. I know my job, and what he expects from me. As one of the oldest players with the most experience under my belt, he expects me to have a leadership role. It's one of the reasons I was given the A on my jersey. I might be known as a quiet and broody guy, but the room listens when I do stand up and say something.

Just before I disappear down the tunnel, I spot Trinity. She's sitting up in the stands, her tripod set up and another camera in her hands. I flash her a smile and wave, waiting a split second to see if she responds. She does, and the smile she gives in return has my heart thudding a little harder in my chest.

I OPEN THE FRIDGE FOR THE THIRD TIME IN A MATTER OF TEN minutes. There still isn't anything in it that looks or sounds appetizing. I give up and decide to head out and grab some dinner. I just have this desire to not be alone. I could call one of the guys, but they aren't who I want to see. The only problem is, the one person I want to have dinner with, I don't have a number for.

An idea pops into my head. I grab my phone and pull up the Instagram app. I find her personal account and before I can stop myself, I hit the message button and start typing.

> Want to go grab dinner? I'd have called or texted, but realized I don't have your number.

I re-read what I sent, and don't know if I should smack myself for sending it to her or praise myself for actually doing so.

My phone chimes a minute later, alerting me to a message notification from Instagram. I quickly click on the notification and open my messages.

> Actually, I'd love to. I haven't felt like cooking and need some food. Also, my number is 555-0143 for future reference.

I copy her number and add it to my contacts, then shoot her a text message, rather than reply on Instagram.

DAMIEN

Hey, this is Damien. Do you want me to come pick you up?

TRINITY

I feel so important, getting Damien Thompson's number. Should I tease the puck bunnies?

Don't make me regret giving it to you. Also, dinner. What's your preference? I'm about to chew my arm off, so make a decision woman.

Bossy much? I guess you can pick me up, or I can meet you, whatever's easier.

Address? And is a steakhouse okay with you? I need some protein after today's practice.

Address link: That sounds good to me, I'm not super picky.

I'll be there in ten.

I grab my keys and wallet and head out to the garage. I decide to take the sports car tonight. It's a fun little car to drive around.

My phone connects via Bluetooth and the GPS pulls up the most direct route to Trinity's place. I somewhat know the area she lives in, which is a good part of town.

I pull in, finding a visitor spot for her building. I press the buzzer for her unit and wait.

"I'm headed down!" her cheery voice comes over the speaker.

"Okay, I'll just wait here then," I tell her as I rock back on my heels.

It doesn't take long before I see her through the window. She's got on some cut off jean shorts and a top that shows off her cleavage. I about swallow my tongue at the sight of her as she walks my way. *Down boy,* I remind my dick.

"Hey, thanks for inviting me out," she says once outside with me.

"Yeah, no problem." I stumble over my own damn words. She's scrambling my brain and I don't really know what to do about that.

"So, are we going to dinner or just standing here?" She chuckles.

"Fuck," I mutter. I'm truly off my game when she's around. "Yeah, let's go," I tell her as I hold up a hand, motioning for her to walk in front of me. That was a mistake. The shorts cup her ass in the most perfect way, making me want to run my hands over the globes and give them a good squeeze as I lift her up and preferably onto my bed.

I walk to the passenger side of my car, and after unlocking the car, I open the door so Trinity can get in.

"Thank you," she says as she sits down. I rake my eyes over her long, bare legs and, once again, have to will my dick to stay down.

I quickly round the car and get in myself. Once buckled, I pull out of the spot and point my car in the direction of the steakhouse I was craving.

"You said something about a steakhouse?" Trinity finally asks, breaking the silence between us.

"It's a little local place, not one of those big chains. I found it when I first came out here after being picked up by the Shock-waves. They have one of the best porterhouses I've ever had."

"Sounds like my kind of place," she says.

"Are you from California?" I ask, realizing I don't know a

whole lot about her other than she likes to take pictures and is damn good at it.

"California, yes, San Francisco, no. I grew up in Anaheim, came up here for a change of scenery. My best friend had moved up here and I followed him after a few months."

"Him?" I find myself questioning.

"Oh, please tell me you aren't one of those people that thinks people of the opposite sex can't be friends. Plus, Michael would be more into you than me. That is, if he wasn't already married to the love of his life, Matteo."

I exhale a breath of relief. "I've only ever heard of times when the relationship ended because one friend had more feelings than the other did, or of cases where they both finally realized they were in love with each other. But your situation sounds solid, as well."

Trinity laughs and it is one of the most beautiful sounds I've heard in a long ass time. "Let me guess, your only female friends are really just the women in your family and those that are in relationships with your male friends."

I grunt because she's hit the nail on the head with that assumption. "I don't really have a lot of friends. Kind of hard to keep relationships going when you only leave the house for work," I find myself confiding in her.

I pull into the parking lot of the restaurant and find a spot near the front to park in. Trinity opens her door at the same time I open mine, so I miss being able to assist her out. We fall into step next to one another and, without even thinking about it, I place my hand on the small of her back. The moment my skin connects with hers, where her top shows off a small strip of skin between the bottom if it and the top of her shorts, has my skin zinging like I was just shocked. A shiver runs through Trinity's body, and it makes me wonder if she felt the same thing as I did.

I pull open the large door as we step through and into the

small foyer. The hostess ready to greet us. "Welcome in tonight, do you have a reservation?" she asks.

"We don't, but I was hoping to get a table for two," I tell her.

"Not a problem, it will be a short wait, maybe five to ten minutes."

"That's fine, can we wait at the bar?" I ask.

"Of course, I'll just give you this and it will buzz when we're ready to seat you," she says as she hands over one of the square buzzers that restaurants use.

"Want a drink while we wait?" I ask Trinity as I lead her to the bar.

"Sure," she says as we take a seat and I pass her a menu from in front of me.

"Evening, I'm Isaiah, what can I get the two of you to drink tonight?" Isaiah asks as he sets two coasters down in front of us.

"I'm still thinking," Trinity says as she looks at the menu.

"I'll take a rum and Coke, please," I tell him.

"Top shelf?" he asks and I nod my agreement.

"I think I'm ready," Trinity says, looking up at Isaiah. "I'll have the Mango Breeze."

"Coming right up," he tells us as he pulls down two glasses and gets to making both drinks.

He sets them down on the coasters. "Did you want to open a tab, or just pay for these now?" he asks. I hand over my credit card since we should be seated soon.

"Cheers," I say, holding up my glass. Trinity picks hers up and clinks it against mine before we both take a drink.

"You didn't have to pay for my drink, I could have paid for it, but thank you."

I can't help but chuckle at her. "Sweetheart, it was noth-ing. And I invited you to join me, I planned on paying whether you liked it or not," I tell her. The term of endear-ment just rolled off my tongue like it was natural to call her that. I always called Kelly sunshine as she was like a ray of sunshine compared to my darkness. I've never had the desire to call another woman by anything other than her name, so that's something I'll definitely be diving further into when I'm back home and alone.

We've only drank about half of our drinks when the square pager starts buzzing. I escort Trinity back to the hostess stand and then to the table the young girl leads us to. They've given us a small little table for two that is in the corner. It is very intimate and offers a bit of privacy thanks to the way it is tucked away.

I let Trinity pick where she'd like to sit before I take the other seat. Our server is already waiting for us as he hands over the large menus.

"Good evening, I'm Dimitri, I'll be taking care of the two of you tonight. I see we already have some drinks from the bar. Are we good with those or would you like to get another order on its way?"

"I'm good for now, except can I get a glass of ice water?" Trinity asks.

"Of course, would you like lemon?"

"No, thank you," she tells him.

"I'm good for now," I say. "Just give us a couple minutes to look over the menu, please."

"Of course," he says before stepping away.

"You've already told me about the porterhouse you love from here, do you have any other recommendations?" Trinity asks me.

"For sides, the Caesar salad is amazing, as are the au Gratin potatoes. Are you a meat kind of girl?"

"I am," she says, and gives me what I think is a flirty smile over her menu.

"The filet is very tender, practically melts in your mouth."

"Perfect, I was looking at that already. Are the sides family style?"

"They are fairly large portions, but they don't say they are, and we could easily get away with sharing one or two."

"What are you craving tonight?" she asks.

You almost slips out, but I catch myself before it does. "The au Gratin potatoes and maybe the grilled mixed vegetables, unless you want something different."

"Both of those sound perfect." Trinity sets her closed menu aside as much as she can, seeing as the table is hardly bigger than a postage stamp.

Dimitri returns with Trinity's water and takes our order, promising to return with a basket of fresh rolls and butter.

"Tell me more about yourself," I prompt once we're alone again.

"Not a whole lot to tell. I grew up in a quintessential upper middle class-family who lived in the suburbs. I was the good girl for most of my childhood, never wanting to get into big trouble and disappoint my parents. Most people at my school probably thought of me as a nerd, but I was far from it. I took photography classes and was on the yearbook. After I graduated, I went to school and got a degree in photography with minors in social media and public relations. I moved to San Francisco about four years ago, and well, as they say, the rest is history."

"Do you have any siblings?"

"Nope, how about you?"

"I have one brother, Connor. He's five years younger than me and lives back home. Is married and they're having their first baby in a few months."

"Congratulations to them. Are you excited to become an uncle?" Trinity asks. I hadn't really thought much about my own excitement.

"Um, am I supposed to be?" I ask, feeling a little foolish.

Trinity laughs, making me not feel like such a dick. "I guess women probably get a little more excited about new babies joining the family than the men do."

"I'd have to agree with you on that one, our mom is ecstatic about the baby."

"Where is back home for you?" Trinity asks.

"You mean, you haven't googled me yet?" I tease. "The suburbs of Minneapolis," I tell her. "Connor and Katie are both dentists. They met while in college together."

"Aww, do they work together, then?" she asks.

"Yes, they started a practice together a few years ago and have grown it into quite the place."

"Do you go back home in the off-season?"

"Not for all of it. I spend a decent chunk of my time up in Canada, training with some old coaches and trainers up there," I tell her, but leave out the part that the coach is also my father-in-law, or ex-father-in-law or whatever in the hell he is to me these days.

"So, if you spend your off-season training, do you ever really get a break?"

"I relax enough. My career is quickly approaching the end. I'm ancient when it comes to hockey players and am lucky to still be playing. Not too many guys make it into their late thirties like I have with minimal injuries. So, until I have to hang up my skates for good, I'll put in the effort to keep myself going all season. It can be a grind. The season is long, even longer if you're lucky enough to make it into the post season, but it's all worth it if you get to hoist up the cup at the end."

"Have you ever won the cup?"

"I thought you stalked my Instagram page," I tease. "But yes, I was lucky enough to be on a cup-winning team early in my career. My second season playing fully up in the NHL, we went all the way and won. It was an exciting time."

"I bet. I'll have to go back and look for some pictures around then."

"I could have sworn I posted some, but maybe I didn't. Hell if I know, that was a long time ago," I tell her.

Dimitri returns with our food, as soon as the smell of the

seasonings hit my nose, my mouth is watering for the first bite. "Still doing okay with drinks or can I get you something else?"

I've finished off my drink. "I'm good with just the one, I'll take some water when you have a minute."

"Of course, enjoy," he says and turns away.

Trinity groans next to me and my cock swells. Thank God for the table hiding what she does to me. "You weren't lying one bit. This is so good," she says just before her lips wrap around the tines of her fork with another bite of the filet.

"I told you it was the best place in town."

We say very little while we both devour our meals. We brush hands as we both reach for the large serving spoon on the potatoes, but I let her take what she wants, first. I can't ignore the zing of electricity I feel every time our bodies connect. It doesn't matter if it's a small brush of skin or us fully touching one another. It's like there's an electrical pull I feel for this woman, but I have no idea where it's coming from.

CHAPTER 10
TRINITY

Damien is different tonight. I'm not sure exactly what it is, but he's different. Everyone on the team jokes about how he's this broody and closed-off guy, but I've never seen that side of him. He's always gone out of his way to make sure I'm good and I find that I like it. I like peeling back his layers, almost like a cinnamon roll. Get past the hard, crunchy outer layers and you'll find the gooey center that is the best part.

When I first started my job, I had to go into it knowing that I was going to be taking pictures of all these guys and most of them are *hot hot hot*—like, it could fulfill any woman's wet dreams for months kind of hot. And now I find myself at a restaurant with who I happen to think is the hottest single guy on the team. Is this a date? Or just friends having dinner together? Don't really know, especially after his spiel earlier about opposite sexes having friends of the opposite gender, and how he doesn't think that works well. But one could also argue it is a date because he picked me up and insisted on buying dinner.

Whatever this evening is, I'm enjoying getting to know Damien better.

"How old were you when you started to play hockey?" I ask Damien once we've both slowed down from eating.

"I was out on skates for as long as I can remember. I think I played on my first team when I was five or so. I know my mom still has the pictures from way back then."

"Aww, I'm sure it was so cute to watch you skate around."

"Something like that." He snickers. "Did you play any sports growing up?"

"I tried a season of soccer, didn't like it. Then moved on to softball, didn't like that, either. Then, in middle school, some of my friends convinced me to try volleyball with them and that was okay, I just wasn't very good at it, so my sports career ended in middle school. When did you decide that going pro was your trajectory in life?"

"By my teens I was being told I had solid talent and had scouts watching me. I went into AAA hockey when I was sixteen, lived with a billet family in Pennsylvania for a season. After that, I was drafted by a Juniors team at seventeen and played juniors for three seasons before I went back home and played for the University of Minnesota. Between eighteen and twenty, you are eligible for the draft, which is different from all other major sports. With hockey, the draft just allows teams to control your professional rights, so to speak. Most of the time, they will have guys continue to develop down in Juniors or with the college they've committed to. Unless you are a protégé player, you won't see the pros until a few years after you are actually drafted. As long as you don't play a game in a league that actually pays you to play, you retain your college eligibility. I played two seasons in college before I secured a spot on an AHL roster after attending their prospect camp."

"Wow, I can't believe you left home so young. That must have been hard on your parents," I tell him.

"My first year away was a big growth year for me. Not only was I away from my parents and friends, but the hockey was intense. There were definitely a few times I had thoughts of do I really want to do this, but in the end, I did. I love hockey and what it has allowed me to do in my life. The people it has brought into my life have been some of the most important people to me. I still consider my billet family good friends."

"And the coaches in Canada must have made an impression if you go back to train with them every summer."

He nods and reaches for his water, taking a large drink before setting it down and speaking again. "One of the coaches I go back to work with is Kelly's dad. He was my coach when I was playing Juniors. It's how I met Kelly."

"You married your coach's daughter?" I ask. "And he didn't kill you?"

Damien chuckles. "He didn't. I was worried he would trade me when he found out we were dating, but he came around to the idea. Gave me a stern lecture about not making him a grandfather while I was playing for him. Said that as long as that didn't happen, and I never hurt his baby girl, then we'd be okay."

"I think that's awesome that you have such a good relationship with them still," I tell him. It is obvious by what he's mentioned about Kelly that they were truly in love and happy. I can also see the hurt or longing in his eyes from how much he misses her.

"They will always be my family. Always," he states. "Any Mr. or Mrs. Rights in your life?" Damien asks.

I can't help but smile and chuckle at his question. "Are you fishing for personal information, Mr. Thompson?" I flutter my lashes at him. I don't miss the way his eyes flash with what I'm confident was desire.

"Something like that, Ms. Black." The way my name rolls off his tongue does something to my insides.

"No relationships to be found. I had one semi-serious boyfriend during college, but it definitely wasn't a relationship that was destined to last. Since then, I've just kissed a bunch of frogs while I search for my Prince Charming. What about you, have you dated since Kelly passed away?" I ask.

"No, I've had—" He pauses and clears his throat like he's uncomfortable with the way this conversation has gone.

"You don't have to answer me, if it's too much, I understand."

"It's not that, I just don't want you to think I'm an asshole," he says behind gritted teeth. I can hear his molars grinding as he pulls in a deep breath, then blows it out slowly.

"I don't think you're an asshole. A grieving man who lost the love of his life, yes. But that doesn't make you an asshole."

He stares into my eyes. So hard that I wouldn't be surprised if he can see all the way to my soul. He must find what he's looking for as his jaw unclenches and he visibly relaxes. "I went through a faze that I'm not proud of. It was the summer after she died. My season ended and I'd just been hanging on by a thread during that time. I'd go to practice, come home, go to games. In between those times, I was usually drunk, just trying to numb the pain. The coaching staff was as accommodating as they could be, but they couldn't just keep me around if I was going to be dead weight. When the season ended, I really fell off the deep end. Was drinking every moment I was awake. Would go to bars and pick up women, just to bring them to a hotel so we could fuck the night away, then leave before morning, never to be heard from again. That lasted maybe six or eight weeks until David, my father-in-law, showed up on my doorstep and smacked some sense into me."

"That doesn't make you an asshole," I tell him as I reach over and place my hand on top of his, trying to give him a small sliver of comfort. "That's how you grieved and dealt with the heartache of losing the love of your life."

"I lost everything that night. My wife, and unborn child," he says, the sadness of the situation hitting me hard.

"She was pregnant?"

"Apparently. We didn't know yet, or at least, I didn't. I don't know if she'd taken a test or not while I was gone. The doctor told me when I arrived at the hospital to say my last goodbyes. It came up on the initial blood work they ran. They could tell from her test that she was early, but it was still just another thing that was taken from me in the blink of an eye."

"I am so sorry," I tell him, not that I can change what happened.

"I didn't mean to talk about such heavy stuff tonight, sorry about that." He turns his hand that is under mine, causing my hand to fall into his palm. He wraps his large hand fully around mine, giving me a few squeezes.

"Any dessert for either of you, tonight?" Dimitri asks, interrupting the moment.

We pull apart, like we just got busted doing something we weren't supposed to be doing, even though that is the furthest from the truth.

"I'm good," I say quickly.

"I don't have any more room." Damien rubs his flat stomach. "I'll take the check when you have a moment."

"Of course, did either of you need a box?" I look between our plates and both of us have pretty much eaten it all.

"I think we're good," I tell him.

"Then I'll be right back with the check."

"Are you sure I can't pay for my portion?" I ask before Dimitri returns.

He just gives me a look, one that says I dare you to pull out your credit card and just see what I do. I'm almost tempted to do it just to get his reaction, but I decided tonight isn't the night to test the bear.

Once Damien gets his card back and has signed the slip, we head back outside. His hand presses against my lower back and the contact sends shivers down my spine. My core clenches with the thought of those rough hands touching me elsewhere. Places that clothes need to come off for him to touch.

He escorts me back out to his car, opening the door for me to get in.

"Thank you," I say before sliding into the car. I don't miss how he watches my every move; I can practically feel his stare on my skin. "Where to now?" I ask as he gets behind the wheel.

"You tell me," he says, and I swear, his voice has dropped an octave.

"Hmmm," I hum, trying to think about where we should go. There is no denying we have a mutual attraction brewing between the two of us, but is it something that we should really act on? I know there isn't a rule prohibiting it at work, but wouldn't that make things weird if our relationship fizzled out. "I don't know, what do you say?" I put it back on him to decide.

He runs a hand through his hair, which draws my attention there and makes me wonder what it would be like to rake my own fingers through it while he's buried deep inside me. I snap back to the present when he grunts. "What thought just went through your mind?" he asks.

I can feel the embarrassment heat my cheeks. "I can't answer that," I whisper.

"You can tell me anything, Trinity," he coaxes.

I shake my head no. "It's way too embarrassing," I say just above a whisper. The only other noise is the low hum of the engine as it idles.

He shifts as much as he can in the driver's seat, so that he's facing me. He cups my cheek with his hand, then slides it back to grip my neck. He tips my head back, so I'm forced to meet his gaze. "Don't ever be embarrassed with me," he says, and I can tell he's thinking just as hard as I am. I don't stop watching him. The way his eyes bounce between my own and my lips multiple times. My tongue sneaks out, wetting my bottom lip, and I swear that is going to break him. "Fuck," he mutters just as he releases my neck and turns back forward in his seat. The car moves ahead as we pull out of the parking spot and out onto the road.

The drive back to my condo is quiet. I glance Damien's way multiple times, but his focus is always on the road, although I can tell he's processing something in that mind of his.

CHAPTER 11
DAMIEN

I pull up to Trinity's condo and park the car. My mind and heart have been racing since we got into the car after dinner. I was so close to leaning down and kissing her. The unwavering want I've all of a sudden developed for this woman is unlike anything I've ever experienced. When I met Kelly, I think it was the thrill of getting caught, since she was supposed to be off limits, being my coach's daughter and all. Not that their relationship had anything to do with our attraction to one another, but there was that layer of deceitfulness in the early days of our relationship.

My pull toward both women can't be compared. I was at very different parts of my life when I met each of them. Now, I just have to tell my heart and brain to get on the same page. Kelly would have wanted me to move on, finding someone new to spend my life with, start a family with. Not that I'm ready for any of those things or am ready to put the cart before the horse, so to speak, but Trinity has me feeling like those things could be a possibility if I can get over my own hesitations.

I shut off the car and get out, rounding the front to open the passenger door for Trinity to get out.

"Thank you again for dinner, I had a great time." She smiles up at me. I can tell she's holding back, and I don't blame the girl. I'm sure the signals I'm throwing at her are confusing as fuck.

"I had a great time. Next time, you can pick the restaurant," I tell her to try and lighten the mood.

"Yeah, maybe," she says before chewing on her bottom lip like she's nervous. "Would you like to come up for a drink?"

I close the few feet between us where we both stand next to my car, forcing her to back up until she's pinned between my body and the car. I place a hand on either side of her, completely boxing her in. "I want nothing more than to do just that, but I don't think tonight is the night. I won't lie, I'm attracted to you and have enjoyed getting to know you. I want to continue to get to know you more. I've lived through hell and back and I don't know what the fuck I'm doing. I just know I want to explore this pull, or connection, or whatever the fuck you want to call what's developing between us and see where it takes us. I also don't want to rush anything."

Trinity rakes her hands up the sides of my torso until her palms are resting on my chest. "You're a good man, Damien. I feel the pull, too. I can't explain it, and I don't really want to. What do we do about work?" she asks.

"Work doesn't matter right now. What matters is you and me."

"I get that, but won't things be weird at work if we're seeing one another?"

"I'm already quiet and broody and can keep things bottled up for a long fucking time. Can you keep your eyes and hands off of me is the better question?" I quirk a brow.

She laughs and it causes her head to tip back, thankfully, not hard enough to crack her head on the car, but it pushes her chest out just enough to press against my own. Her hands fall back to my sides, and I can't miss the feeling of her pert nipples pressing into my chest. Just as she can't miss my hard cock pressed against her stomach.

"Let me walk you to your door," I whisper into her ear. I press a kiss just underneath it and love the way her skin puckers under my lips. I can feel the thrum of her heartbeat as my lips skim down the column of her neck until I pull away and grab her hands with my own.

"Okay," she breathily answers, and my cock presses even harder against my zipper. She interlocks our fingers together as we walk across the parking lot and into the lobby of her building. The elevator ride up is short, as is the walk down the hall to her door.

Trinity turns to face me once we reach her door. "You sure you want to go?" she asks, clearly not wanting me to leave.

"I'm not sure of anything," I tell her honestly.

"Just a drink?" she offers again.

"You make it hard for a man to say no."

"Then don't," she says, and turns to unlock the door. She opens it and steps over the threshold, turning to look at me over her shoulder. "Are you coming?" she asks, and that's my undoing.

I push the door all the way open and step in behind her and close the door. I follow her into the living room. I don't pay much attention to the surroundings, just keep my focus on Trinity until we stop in the middle of the room.

I grip her hip, tugging her until our bodies are pressed flush against one another. My cock pulses as it's trapped against the zipper. "You're so fucking beautiful," I tell her as I cup her face with my free hand. My thumb rubs against those kissable lips, and the little vixen flicks her tongue out as the pad of my thumb brushes back over her bottom lip. I feel that flick all the way down to the tip of my crown, she might as well have done it there. "Tell me to stop if you don't want me to kiss you right now, Trinity," I tell her as I slowly lower my head.

She says nothing, but slowly presses up on her toes, closing the distance between us quicker than I was. Our lips meet for the first time, and I feel like I'm floating, like this is a dream that I never want to wake up from. I open up, sliding my tongue along the seam of her lips, asking for her to open up for me. She does and I deepen the kiss, our tongues tangle as we both take and take as we explore one another.

I take the hand gripping her hip and slide my arm fully around her midsection, giving me the leverage I need to pick her up. Without stopping our kiss, I stumble the few feet to the wall, thankfully, it's bare and I'm able to pin her up against it. Trinity wraps her legs around my waist, giving me the perfect opportunity to grind my cock against her center. Her fingers rake through my hair, the scrape of her nails against my skin send shockwaves down my spine and into my balls.

I slow the kiss, enjoying lazily kissing her into a frenzied state. I pull back completely, then press a kiss at the corner of her mouth as we both suck in much needed air. "You're going to be the death of me," I tell her as I lean my forehead against hers.

"No, I won't, but I might become the stealer of all your kisses," she says as she pulls my head until our lips connect once more.

We kiss and grind against one another like two horny teenagers. Time feels like it stands still. We break apart, Trinity needing to be set back down on the floor.

"Still want that drink?" she asks once her feet are firmly planted back on the floor. She looks up at me with a sexy smile on her kiss-swollen lips.

I chuckle, knowing that offering me a drink was just a ruse to get me inside. Not that I'm complaining or that I was hard to convince to come in.

"Not tonight," I say as I reach out and tuck a lock of hair

behind her ear. "But can I have a rain check?" I ask as I cup her chin and run my thumb across her lips.

"Of course," she says, but doesn't break our connection.

"As much as it pains me, I'm going to go. There's no reason for us to rush this. I don't know that I'm ready to rush things, if I'm being honest, and that is something that I will always be with you. I don't want to play games, Trinity. I won't lead you on, and I can only ask that you'd give me the same courtesy."

"Of course," she agrees. "Thank you for tonight."

"You're welcome, Sweetheart," I say before I press a kiss to her forehead. "Lock up after I leave. I'll see you tomorrow." I tug her into a hug, loving the feeling of our bodies pressed together. It kills me to do so, but I finally let go and step back. She wraps her arms around her torso like she's giving herself a hug.

I walk backwards down the little hallway until I'm a step away from the door. "Night," I say before I turn and open the door and walk out, shutting it behind me.

CHAPTER 12
TRINITY

I stand in the hallway, staring at the closed door. My mind reels at tonight's events. I still can't believe what transpired. From the message on Instagram to Damien pinning me up against the wall and kissing me like our lives depended on it.

"Lock the door, Trinity." I hear his deep voice rumble through the door. I sprint into action, closing the distance to the door and turning the lock. "Good girl. I'll see you tomorrow," he says. I peek at him through the peep hole and watch as he turns and walks down the hall. I turn so my back is against the door and sink down until my ass hits the floor. I grab my phone from my back pocket and hit Michael's name as soon as my phone is unlocked.

"Hello," he greets, and I can hear the TV on in the background.

"Am I interrupting anything?" I ask.

"Just watching some re-runs of some house hunting show. It's all so staged and fake, but I can't stop watching," he says. "What are you up to tonight?"

"I don't even know where to start," I admit to him.

"How about the beginning?" he suggests. "And I'm going

out on a limb that everything is okay based on no tears or hysteria."

"Everything is perfect," I tell him. "I was putzing around, trying to decide what I wanted for dinner, when I got a notification that someone had slid into my DMs on Instagram. When I checked it, I had a message from Damien Thompson, one of the defensemen. He was the one that helped me when I had my card issues when we went to Seattle last week."

"I remember who he is, I also googled him, he's a fucking knockout, so go on," Michael says.

"Anyways, he slid into my DMs and asked if I wanted to go to dinner with him. I, of course, said yes and ten minutes later he was here picking me up. We went to this little steakhouse that was so good. You and Matteo need to try it out. But anyways, back to my evening. We had a drink at the bar while we waited for a table, chatted a little, then got seated at this small little table in the corner. We talked all throughout dinner, just getting to know one another better. He was married a while ago, but his wife died in a car accident. That's had him pretty messed up for a while, so I think he's scared to move on. I think he feels like he's dismissing her if he does, which is so sad, but also honorable at the same time."

"It would be such a disservice to mankind if he doesn't reproduce. That man is S-E-X on legs. Please tell me the evening got even friskier," Michael says and I can't help but laugh.

"When he walked me back to his car, he placed his hand against my lower back to escort me, which he'd done earlier when we went inside, but there was just something about this time. Maybe because his fingers splayed across my bare skin, but it caused my body to hum with anticipation. By the time we made it to the car, the tension between us was strong. After we got into the car, he almost kissed me but pulled away and he drove me back home in silence. Once we got here, and we were out of the car, he pinned me against it and almost kissed me again. It was so hot, but the restraint it took not to just kiss him was something else." I sigh, just remembering what it felt like to have his body under my palms, and that was even with the layers of clothes between us.

"Damn, girl; I'm fanning myself from across town," Micheal says. "Keep going."

"He'd asked to walk me to my door, and I agreed, even though I'd been asking him if he wanted to come in for a drink."

"You go, girl," he interjects.

"We made it to my door, and let's just say, I convinced him to come in. We kissed for a few minutes and then he lifted me up and pinned me to the wall. It was seriously the best kiss I've ever had. His body was so hard *everywhere,* and damn, the way it pressed against mine was everything. I'm just pissed there were clothes between us."

"Ok, but when do we get to the dirty?" he asks, all impatient.

"Not tonight," I tell him, not bothering with letting him down easy. "He eventually stepped back and gave me a little spiel about how he wants to take things slow. He's not ready to rush anything, which I believe one hundred percent. I actually think it would make him close up if we rushed anything too soon. We've talked a decent amount, and I know from those talks that he's just now coming around to the idea of dating again."

"So do you have another date planned or what?" he asks.

"No, but I'll see him at work tomorrow. That's another thing I worry about. What will it look like if the new girl is hooking up with a player before the season even officially starts?"

"Are there any rules against it?" Michael asks.

"No there aren't."

"Then you don't have to worry about being fired if you were to date him, so my advice is to have fun. See where things go, or don't. Have all the dirty fun sex, because let's face it, the man has got to have some stamina with the kind of job he does. As long as he makes you happy and puts you first, I say follow your heart."

"When he left, he told me to lock up behind him. I stood staring at the door for a couple of minutes, just soaking in everything that had transpired, but then he was talking to me through the door, telling me to lock it. As soon as he heard the click of the lock turning, he told me I was a good girl. Michael, I think I have a praise kink because of him saying that. Oh oh, and he called me Sweetheart a couple of times tonight and it was fucking swoon worthy. Like, melted my panties on the spot."

"He's got it baaaad," Michael sing-songs. "But then again, so do you." He chuckles.

"Has Trinity bagged a hockey player yet?" I hear Matteo ask from the background and I fall into a fit of giggles.

"She's working on it, Honey. They made out like two teenagers tonight."

"When do we get to meet him and give our seal of approval?" Matteo asks, his voice getting louder as he must be getting closer to Michael's phone.

"Um, I'll have to get back to you on that," I tell him. "We're taking things slow, very slow, so that might have to wait a few weeks or months."

"We'll be here when you're ready," Matteo tells me. "You know we love you and we just want the best for you."

"I know. You guys are the best ever," I tell them and truly mean it.

"All right, keep me posted. Call me tomorrow when you get out of work and update me on how he acts around you."

"Will do," I tell him before we say our goodbyes and hang up.

I finally stand up from the entryway floor, brushing off my butt once I'm standing. It's getting late, so I head for the bathroom so I can get ready for bed. I wash my face, getting all the makeup off from today, then moisturize before brushing my teeth. I slip out of my shorts and top and into a baggy t-shirt. I slip beneath the sheets and wish Damien was here with me. What would it feel like to have him hovering over me, that large body of his could deliver so much pleasure for both of us.

Did you make it home?

I did, and I'm already in bed.

I'm also in bed.

Fuck, wish I hadn't walked out when I did.

Don't second guess your in the moment decisions, they are usually for the best. Taking this slow is the right thing to do. I don't want you to get spooked or feel like things are being rushed.

I'm good, I promise.

I'm glad. See you tomorrow :winky face:

Good night, sleep well.

I have a short date with my book boyfriend until I fall asleep.

Book boyfriend? Should I be jealous?

Maybe :shrugging emoji: He's quite swoony. If only real men were this smooth in real life. :fans self:

Pfff, I could show this cock sucker up any day of the week.

Exaggerating laughing emoji: He's only fictional. No need to get your hackles up. But if you want me to send you some of the spicy scenes to role play, I'm happy to do so. :winky emoji:

Send them my way, I'll be happy to oblige.

I'll look for a good one, this author tends to be pretty descriptive with her spicy scenes. They are :chef kiss: amazing!

Do they make you wet and horny?

All the time. My vibrator gets quite the workout.

I can't believe I just told you that. In a text message. Just kill me now.

Seriously, I'm going to roll over and die of embarrassment.

There's nothing to be embarrassed about. Self pleasure is very normal. That's not to say I wouldn't want the chance to also help you out in that department.

If it helps take away any of the embarrassment, I've gotten quite good at taking care of my own needs. I could show you sometime. :winky face:

You still there or did I lose you?

I'm still here, just trying to come back from my embarrassment.

Okay, as long as I didn't scare you away. But on that note, I'll let you get back to your book. Good night, Trinity. I had a great time tonight. Thank you for pulling me out of my own head.

I read over his last text. I know he wants to give credit to others for his newfound desire to get back out there, but that all has to come from him. He has to be the one that wants it and makes the effort. I can just hope his desire continues and I'm included in that.

CHAPTER 13
DAMIEN

I walk into the rink, my suit looking just right as I strut down the hallway. I round the corner and see Trinity set up at the end of the hall with her cameras. I can't hold back the smile that fills my face when I see her. She looks gorgeous sitting on the stool, her long hair pulled back in a ponytail that rests high on her head. She's dressed in slacks and a team polo that does nothing to hide her curves.

I smirk as I get closer to her camera and flash her a wink as I round the corner into the dressing room. I catch a glimpse of her cheeks as they tinge pink before I disappear behind the door. I'm sure that footage will give her some good post material.

"My man, you ready for tonight?" Tristan asks as I take a seat next to him in my stall. We're placed right next to one another in the locker room since we're partners out on the ice. I bump his outstretched fist, as we've done now since our first game together.

"I'm ready to kick some ass. Get this season off on a good foot," I tell him.

"That's the attitude!" Ryker exclaims as he walks past us. I watch as he strides around the room, pumping everyone up.

He's the perfect guy to be the captain of this team. The fire he has for this game and the drive he has to lead this team is like nothing I've ever experienced from any other captain I've played with.

Everyone disperses as we get a move on our pre-game rituals. There is so much more to the game than the actual sixty minutes of regulation.

"Are you ready for the first home game of the regular season?" I ask Trinity when I see her waiting in the hallway. It's almost time for us to hit the ice for warmups, and I can already hear the rumble of the crowd. I'm sure it isn't even full yet out in the stands, but the people that are in here already are loud and ready for the season to start.

"I think so. I have a feeling it's going to be crazy tonight," she says.

"I think you're right."

"I'll see you later, I need to go take my place." She flashes me a quick smile. One I'd like to think was just for me. I watch her walk away, only realizing I'm staring at her when Tristan busts me for it.

"See something you like?" he asks, smacking my chest protector with the back of his gloved hand.

I turn to face him, no expression on my face, but he must be able to read me like a fucking book, because he calls me on it, once again.

"Damn, bro, you've got it bad. Does she know?" he asks.

"We've been talking. Went out on a date, but we're taking it slow," I admit.

"She seems nice."

"Yep," I give him a short, one-word answer.

"She must be a saint if she's willing to put up with your broody ass. Hopefully, you give her more than one-word answers and grunts," he teases.

I grunt a reply, which does nothing but make him hunch

over laughing. "I talk to her, asshole," I finally tell him. "I don't think I've ever grunted at her."

"So, you only save that for the guys, then? I see how it is."

"Fuck off," I tell him, but there isn't any heat behind my words.

We get the signal that it is time to go. Blake leads us down the tunnel and out onto the ice. Trinity is positioned on the bench, capturing all of us as we get to work.

The roar of the crowd pumps me up as soon as my skates hit the frozen surface. I circle around our half of the ice, warming up my legs and getting the blood pumping.

Our twenty or so minutes of warmups fly by, and before I know it, I'm headed back down the tunnel for the locker room. One of the radio people pull me aside, asking for a quick interview before the game starts. I take my helmet off and slip the headset on, adjusting the microphone so they can hear me.

"Thanks for a few minutes of your time, Damien. Can you tell us what you're looking forward to this season?" I hear through the earpiece.

"No problem. I'm looking forward to another chance to come together as a team and fight our way to the ultimate prize. We've picked up some great players in the off season, and I can't wait to see what they bring to this team."

"New talent is always a good thing, how are you personally feeling? I know you've been playing in this league for a long time, the longest of any player on the roster, how does that make you feel and what kind of encouragement have you passed on to your teammates?"

"I don't take any season for granted that I'm able to play. I try not to think of my age, especially compared to how young some of the new guys are," I tell him, chuckling at the age gap. "I haven't given them any speeches yet; I leave that up to Ryker. He's the one full of advice and wisdom."

He chuckles. "Thanks again for your time tonight,

Damien. Good luck out there," he says and I slip the headset off and push my way into the locker room.

Coach walks into the locker room and all attention is on him. "I don't need to tell any of you how this is a fresh start. A new set of eighty-two games. All it takes is one shift, one period, one game, one win at a time to reach our goal. Stay focused. Do what we've practiced. Clean passes. Shut down their passing and shooting lanes. Tie them up in the corners. Take the shot. We have the talent. We have the drive, now go out there and fucking win our first game of the season," he says excitingly. The guys all cheer at his words.

Ian, the head equipment manager, steps forward, a paper in his hand to read from. "Your starting lineup tonight is..." he says all dramatically. Everyone whoops and hollers as we build up the excitement for the game. "Your forward line, led by none other than your captain, Ryker Jorgensen, Aiden Fox, and Jason Soaps," he says, and everyone hoops once again before he can continue. "On defense, we've got the dream team, our oldies—Tristan Henderson and Damien Thompson."

"Hey, who you calling old?" Tristan shouts out, only for all the guys to laugh.

"You need some cream for that burn?" someone calls out.

"And between the pipes. We've got the brick wall... Blake Watson!" Ian finishes the lineup and everyone mills around as the final moments pass that leads us to the opening game of the season.

Blake leads us down the tunnel, stopping just before it ends and the bench opens up. He waits for the cue from the PA announcer, and as soon as that happens, we're moving once again. Most guys just file onto the bench, while those of us on the starting shift take the ice. I skate a few circle-eights just to get the blood pumping. We line up along the blue line for the anthem, and then it's time for the puck to drop.

It's halfway through the second period, we're still tied at

zero when I drill my shoulder into one of LA's defenseman's chests, hitting him hard against the glass. The crowd reacts, liking the hit I just laid out on him. I can't help but smile, since it did what I wanted it to, and that is free up the puck. I swing it along the boards, where Ryker is waiting. He passes the puck forward, right onto the tape of Soapy's stick, where he's at in the neutral zone. I skate hard, flying into our offensive zone behind my teammates. Soapy skates the puck down and behind LA's goal, coming back up the other side. He passes the puck up to the point where Tristan is waiting for it. He winds back and smacks the puck with one hell of a shot. The puck goes flying in the air. A few feet in front of the net, it ricochets off Aiden's stick and finds the back of the net.

"Fucking A," Tristan yells as the crowd goes wild and the goal horn blares in the building. We all come together in our huddle before we return to the bench for fist bumps from the rest of the team. Once through the line, I jump over the boards and take a seat on the bench. I guzzle some water as I catch my breath after that shift. It was intense, but at least we're up on the board where it counts most.

The third period comes in just as fast. LA must have had quite the ass chewing during the second intermission as they come out determined not to get shut out.

I'm on the bench watching the play as it unfolds in front of me, always trying to figure out what they've got up their sleeve. One of their centers poke checks the puck away from our defenseman, pushing it out into the neutral zone. He puts on the jets and skates out, getting himself a nice little breakaway. He takes the puck down, skates wide, then pulls the puck along his backhand as he crosses in front of Blake. He waits him out, and as soon as Blake commits, he flicks it over his pads and into the back of the net.

LA's bench goes wild as they tie up the game with less than five minutes left on the clock. "Listen up," Coach calls out as the LA guys skate to their bench to do the same thing we did when we scored. "Remember what I said before the game. One shift. One goal. One game. You've got four minutes and twenty-nine seconds to close this game out and put two points in the standings. Let's fucking make it happen," he says as a new set of guys take the ice.

The puck drops at center ice and the seconds tick by. We gain control, and Coach taps Tristan and me on the shoulder, his signal that he wants us back out on the ice. As soon as the guys on the ice see that Coach is signaling for a line change and they have the opening, we swap out.

Ryker gathers the puck deep in the zone, but quickly gets swarmed by LA's players. He digs and digs at the puck, attempting to free it up and get it passed out to someone else. Soapy skates down to help him out and jabs the tip of his stick between all the skates that are digging at it, freeing it just enough that he can send it cross ice where I'm wide open and waiting. I skate forward, just waiting for the perfect moment to shoot the puck, I think that moment happens, so I release. Unfortunately for me, their goalie reacts and kicks out his leg at the last second, sending the puck wide. Aiden is there, waiting for it, and crashes the net with the puck once again. Soapy and I follow him in, crashing it, as well, as we all attempt to connect with the puck. I have no idea whose stick connects with it, all I know next is the ref is signaling a goal and the place erupts as the goal lights flash and the horn sounds.

"That's what I'm talking about," I shout as we all huddle around. I look up to the Jumbotron to watch the replay to see if I can determine who actually got the goal. I'm shocked when the PA announcer calls out my name as who tapped it home. I'll fucking take it.

CHAPTER 14
TRINITY

I stay down at ice level the entire game, mostly hanging out in the corners of the rink where the most space is available for media. I'm constantly switching between still shots and video clips, making sure to post the footage of the goals to social media within a few minutes of them happening. The comments are flooding in from all of our posts today.

After the guys arrived this afternoon, I spent some time editing their arrival videos and got one posted to our TikTok page. If my notifications are correct, I think we've gone viral. That damn wink from Damien probably sent the women overboard.

The excitement of the fans is like nothing else. They are hyped to be here tonight, especially since the team has just taken the lead back with a little over a minute left in the game.

As soon as the puck drops after Damien's goal, LA takes possession of the puck and drives it hard down into the zone. As soon as they do, their goalie leaves his crease, heading for the bench. An extra player jumps over the boards and goes down to join the other players. My eyes bounce between the clock on the scoreboard and the ice. Thirty seconds of six on five with an open net.

LA passes the puck between three players all hovering near the blue line. Aiden and Tristan skate between them, trying to close up the passing lane, but miss the first four passes. I glance back up at the clock, they've burned off ten seconds in what feels like ten minutes. One of the LA players attempts to pass the puck down low to one of the guys near the net, but Jason Soaps intercepts the pass and shoots it out of the zone, sending it sailing down to the other end. It looks like it's going to go into the net, but it hits the post and bounces out wide. The crowd collectively groans as the guys all skate as hard as they can down toward LA's net. Aiden beats everyone to the puck that is now behind the net. Their goalie is still pulled, so he passes up to Jason, who's now in front of it with an LA defenseman attempting to block the open space. He shoots the puck, and it sails right past the player just as the buzzer sounds.

We won! Three to one, with a buzzer-beater extra goal. I head out onto the ice, capturing the celebration of the first win of the season. Everyone piles around Blake, giving him the credit he deserves for tonight's win. He had some crazy good saves, and really shined.

"Nice goal," I say to Damien as he skates up next to me. The smile on his face is good to see on him.

"Thanks." He looks down at me. He's already a good head and shoulders taller than me without skates on, so I find myself having to crank my neck back to look up at him with them on. "Did you enjoy the game?"

"I did, it was so much more intense than the pre-season games."

"Yep, that's normal. But expect that from here on out," he tells me. "I gotta go, but talk later?"

"Yeah," I tell him before he skates off the ice. I step into the bench area, my camera ready for the three stars of the game announcement. They each are given a souvenir stick to sign and then give to a fan over the glass. Most of the guys pick out a kid to give it to, so I capture those moments as the three guys come out. Damien as the third star, Tristan as the second, and Blake as the first.

Once the three stars are finished, it is amazing how quickly the arena empties out from the spectators. I understand it is getting late and people are tired. As it quiets down, I realize just how exhausted I am.

I walk down the tunnel and head for my office to plug in all my equipment and gather my bag. I'll take home the memory cards, that way I can work from home tomorrow since there isn't another game.

"The footage online looks excellent," the team's owner, Nathan Bailey, says as he stands at my open doorway. I had the pleasure of meeting him earlier this week. His wife, Harper, was also with him and she was just the sweetest person I've ever met.

"Thank you! The feedback from fans has been great, as well. They are loving all the behind-the-scenes footage I've been posting."

"That's great. Keep giving them what they want. The ticket office says our inquiries for season tickets has gone up, and when they ask people what made them call, a significant number have said from all the ways we've been connecting with them on social media."

"That's great to hear!" I tell him. I didn't expect my work to have that kind of an effect on the team, but I'll take it.

"Whatever ideas you have that you think might work, you have free rein to post them."

"I appreciate the creative freedom and trust you've put in me."

"We only hire the best around here." He gives me a big smile.

"I want to start filming a day-in-the-life-type documentary. Pick a different player each week, maybe, and get clips of them throughout an entire day. Both practice days and game days, then edit the footage down into a five-to-ten-minute mini-documentary."

"I love the idea. Talk to Coach and he'll get you moving forward with it."

"I was thinking I could have the guys film little clips on their own phones of their routines at home, or I can send them with one of my cameras," I explain.

"You figure out what will work best and I'm sure it will turn out great."

"Thanks, Mr. Bailey," I tell him.

"Call me Nathan. Mr. Bailey is my father," he chuckles.

"Ready to go, dear?" Harper walks up and asks him. "Oh, hello, Trinity. It's great to see you tonight."

"Thank you, good to see you. How are you doing tonight?" I ask.

Harper rubs at her very large stomach. "Tired. Ready for this baby to get out and stop using my bladder as a trampoline, but otherwise, I can't complain."

"She'll be here before we know it," Nathan tells her.

"I can only imagine how miserable that must be. How much longer do you have?" I ask.

"My due date is this coming week, but you never know when babies are going to make their entrance, so hopefully by the end of next week. If I'm still pregnant next Friday, I'll be begging my doctor to do whatever he needs to do to evict this little girl. She's had enough time." Harper laughs.

"Aww, she'll be here so soon. Are you all ready?"

"As ready as we can be," Nathan says. "The nursery is all done, our hospital bags are packed, and our mothers are already here, waiting to take over grandma duty as soon as she makes her appearance."

"That's so nice they are both here to help you guys."

"It will be nice once she's born. Until then, they might be

driving me a little crazy. They might have been the real reason I came to the game tonight with Nathan. That, and the unlimited chips and queso we had in the suite."

"Ah, I'm a sucker for some good queso myself," I tell her.

"All right, we'll let you get going," Nathan says as he places a hand on his wife's back. I watch as he escorts her away. They seem like such an awesome couple, very much in love with each other.

Once they are gone, I make sure all my equipment is plugged in and charging, place my MacBook in my shoulder bag, along with the memory cards I used tonight. After one last look around my office, I flip the light off as I make my way out into the hallway and down to the staff parking lot.

As soon as I get home, I strip out of my work clothes and put on a baggy t-shirt and a pair of sleep shorts. I scrub my makeup off and toss my hair up into a messy bun.

It's amazing what some good comfy clothes, sans bra, and a clean face can do to help relax you. I kick back in my recliner, popping my feet up as I flip the TV on. I land on some random cooking show for background noise and pull out my MacBook. I insert the memory card from my camera, first, and download all the images. I've created a system for saving everything; pretty simple, I have folders for practice vs game day footage, then just save it by the date.

Once everything is downloaded, I flip through it, deleting out the images that are truly trash. So many that are completely out of focus, something photobombing my intended target, things like that. Even with deleting images, I still have a few thousand from just tonight.

I pick some favorites and start editing them. I'll use them in the next few days to make some social media content.

I'm just about ready to call it a night when my phone vibrates on the armrest next to me. I flip it over and see Damien's face flashing on my screen.

"Hello," I greet, a little giddy that he's calling me.

"Did I wake you?" he asks.

"No, I just finished editing some pictures."

"Good, now open your door," he says.

"What?" I say, his words catching me off guard.

"Open your door," he says again.

I place my MacBook on the end table and stand up. I limp a little bit due to one of my feet falling asleep, it starts to tingle as I make my way over to the door. I look out the peephole and see him standing there in his suit, button down shirt undone at the top and his tie is missing. I flip the lock and pull the door open, shocked that he's standing there.

"I missed you," he says. He places his phone into his inner suit pocket before stepping forward and gripping me by the hips.

Damien backs me up far enough so the door can close behind him, then turns us and pins me against the wall. "I've been thinking all night about kissing you. Tasting you," he says as his mouth drops to mine. He captures my lips in a kiss, immediately taking possession, my body eager to fall to his control. I slide my hands behind his neck, my fingers sliding along his scalp and into his hair.

He pulls back after a scorching kiss, my body practically deprived of oxygen from it. "God you're beautiful," he says as his eyes rake down my body. I look down and remember that I'm in sleep clothes, nothing sexy about them.

"Not my finest," I admit.

"Don't do that, don't put yourself down. I like seeing you like this. Comfortable and all natural. You've never looked more beautiful."

"Who knew you'd be such a charmer?" I tease.

"I can be so much more." He nips at my ear and my body hums for him. I arch my back, thrusting my chest into his. Without a bra adding a barrier, there is no way he doesn't feel my hard nipples.

"Is that so." I quirk a brow at him, seeing how easy it will be to make him let me in further than he has. It's been weeks since the last time he was here at my apartment. We've talked most of those days, but this is the first time he's just showed up.

Damien cups my cheek, drawing my head up to make eye contact. He rubs his thumb along my bottom lip, like he did that one night. Just like then, I lick it as it passes by. The heat that flashes in his eyes when my tongue connects with his thumb tells me he's ready to let that wall fall down. He wants me, at least, right now he does. "I've craved you since that night. I had to work through some things, but I'm ready now. I want you. Want an us. You've wormed your way into my world by being the friend I didn't know I needed. I'm here to ask you if that's what you want." His voice is gruff and oh-so-sexy. My panties are ready to fall at his feet if I'm not careful.

"Yes," I say, and before I can say anything else, he's picking me up and kissing me hard once again.

He pulls back when we've reached the end of the hall. If you turn right, you end up in the living room and or kitchen, which is really the only part of my condo he's been in. "Bedroom or living room?" he asks.

"Hmmm." I pretend to think about the question, and he retaliates by tickling my sides.

"Damien," I laugh-scream as I squirm.

"I'm going to spank you for that." He nips at my jaw.

"Yes, please." I moan. "Bedroom is through the second door," I tell him. He turns that way and closes the distance quickly. I reach behind me and push the door open. Thankfully, I actually made my bed this morning and when I got home, I didn't just toss my clothes all over it like I usually do. He walks deeper into the room, depositing me on the edge of the bed.

"What are we doing tonight?" he asks, and at first, I'm a little confused by his question. He must notice as he smirks a little before adding to his question. "How fast or slow are we taking things?"

"Hmm." I stand up, positioning our bodies so they're flush against each other. His cock is hard and throbbing behind the zipper of his slacks. "I think we're both just as needy and ready for something a little sweaty and intimate." I rub my hand over the bulge in his pants and he sucks in a breath.

"Fucking hell," he mutters as he grips my wrist. "Sweetheart, you can't touch much tonight or else I'll blow just standing here fully clothed. It's been a while, so I might have to take a few rounds to build my stamina up to a satisfactory level."

"I'm up for the challenge," I tease. I reach for the hem of my t-shirt and pull it up and over my head.

"Fuck," he mutters again. I'm starting to think it's his favorite word with the number of times I've heard him say it. He drops to his knees, then looks up at me with his smoldering gaze. "I'm going to enjoy you, first."

Damien pushes me back onto the bed, and in one quick move, takes my shorts off. He trails a finger down the front of my thong, feeling the wetness building between my legs.

"So wet," he murmurs as he leans forward and kisses me. He slides the string aside and rubs a finger over my swollen clit.

"Yes," I pant into his mouth, my lower body arching off the bed, searching for more contact. I'm already so needy and ready to come and he's hardly touched me yet.

His fingers glide down, finding my entrance. He slides one finger in and my body clenches around it, not wanting to let go. When he pulls back, he pushes two fingers in, stretching me further. The intrusion of his fingers has me dreaming about taking his cock. "Who's a needy girl, now?" he asks, which just pulls a moan from my lips.

Damien moves from kissing my lips to kissing down my

body. He sucks a nipple into his mouth, flicking my it with the tip of his tongue as he rolls the other one with his fingers. The strumming of my clit at the same time has my body tingling as my orgasm builds.

"Come for me, Sweetheart," Damien says as he pulls away from my breast and continues to kiss his way down my torso. When he reaches between my legs, his tongue swirls around my clit, all while his fingers don't let up the pressure they're creating from the inside. The moment he sucks my clit into his mouth, I detonate. My orgasm racks my body. I go rigid for a few seconds, then completely limp. Damien is still lapping at my clit, his fingers slowing their movement as I come down from my high.

"That was beautiful, but now it's time for number two," he says as he completely removes my thong. I watch as he slides off the bed and strips out of his suit. The way this man is fit is mind boggling. The corded muscles in his arms are sexy, but the rest of his body is a true work of art.

Once naked, he tosses the foil packet from his wallet onto the bed next to me. I watch his every move, the way he wraps his fist around his cock and gives it a few strokes. He watches me as his hand works up and down his thick shaft. I swallow hard, wondering just how I'll fit all of him.

"What are you thinking?" he asks as he steps closer to the edge of the bed.

"How you're going to fit," I tell him honestly.

Damien laughs, and even the grittiness of his laugh turns me on. I've now had that scruffy face between my thighs and damn did it feel good. "Sweetheart, you'll take every inch like the good girl that you are." He flashes me a wicked grin as he kneels on the bed. He reaches for the condom and tears the packet open. I watch with care as he rolls the condom down his length, then gives himself a few more strokes. I reach a hand out and cover his, wanting to get my own hands on him. He lets me take over stroking him, his breathing hitching slightly when I tease around his crown. "Fuck, that feels amazing," he groans. I sit up, moving closer to him so I can reach his lips. I don't care that he was just down on me, I kiss him hard, slipping my tongue into his mouth and dueling with his. We make out as I move my body until I'm straddling his lap. His cock slides through my folds, the tip teasing my clit as I slide against it. "I need to be inside you," he pulls back from the kiss to tell me.

I push his upper body back on the bed, his head hitting my pillow. I push up on my shins, giving me the space I need to grip his cock and align it with my opening. I take in his tip, which spreads me wide around him. It feels tight but doesn't hurt. I bounce some, taking in a little more each time I come down. "You're going to kill me," he groans. Damien brings his hands up my sides until he cups my breasts. He plays with my nipples, twisting and flicking them. I finally slide all the way down until my ass is touching his balls.

"Holy hell," I pant. "I'm so full." He moves his hands to my hips and helps my body as I start to bounce up and down. I come up until just the tip is in, and drop down, taking every last inch of him. My orgasm builds quickly, the way my body tingles and comes alive is like nothing I've experienced before. It's never been this good or quick.

Damien shifts a hand, bringing it to my center, and starts circling my clit. The moment he presses against it, I detonate. I shudder, my body going rigid as the orgasm races through me. He thrusts up as my orgasm continues to squeeze his cock.

He cries out when his own orgasm finally explodes. Even with the condom, I can feel the jets of his cum filling it. I collapse forward, my upper body covering his. It takes me a few moments to realize his hands are caressing my back as we both bask in our orgasms.

I roll my head from where my cheek rests on his chest until my chin is resting on it and I can look up at his face.

"That was amazing," I tell him as I feel his cock start to slip out of me.

"I have to agree." He smiles at me. "Let me get up and take care of things." He taps my hip and I slide off of him.

"The bathroom is through the closet," I tell him as I point in the direction of my walk in.

He disappears into the bathroom while I just stay put on the bed. I hear the toilet flush, followed by the sink turning on. "Where do you have clean washcloths?" he asks from the doorway.

"There should be some on the bottom shelf in the little closet in there," I instruct.

The water turns on again and, moments later, he's returning with a warm wet washcloth. He wipes my thighs, then my center. "Did I miss anywhere?" he asks. The way he takes care of me is a little shocking. I've never had a man think about aftercare.

"I'm good, I should still go in and use the bathroom. Even with a condom, I don't want to risk a UTI."

He grabs my hands and pulls me up. "You sure know how to bring a guy out of his shell," he says before kissing me gently. I rest my hands on his bare chest and can feel the way his heart pounds hard against his chest wall. "Go clean up, I'll be waiting for you here," he tells me. I look over my shoulder at him as I step away, giving him a satisfied smile as I go. He reaches out and smacks my ass and I can't help but giggle as I go.

CHAPTER 15
DAMIEN

I slip my boxer briefs back, adjust my half-hard cock and plop back down on the bed, making myself comfortable on one of the pillows. I'm still hot from our activities, so I don't mess with the blankets. I can't imagine she'd kick me out, but I also don't want to just assume anything either.

The moment I saw her after she opened the door, my mind went wild. I had this guttural desire to strip her bare and make her mine.

The light from the bathroom that is filtering through the closet flips off, so I turn my attention in that direction. Trinity saunters to the doorway and I don't know if I've seen a sexier sight. She's still naked and isn't shy about it. Not that I'm comparing Kelly to Trinity, but it took me months to convince Kelly that I loved her body, and she had nothing to be ashamed of.

"You excited to see me?" Trinity asks, quirking a brow and pointing toward my crotch. I can feel my dick getting harder, especially under her scrutiny.

"Always, I'm surprised you never noticed the bulge in my pants when I'm around you."

"Oh, I notice." She flashes me a smirk.

"Get your sexy ass over here," I growl.

The little vixen saunters her way over to the bed, then slowly lowers herself onto the edge, then slides over until she's laying next to me on her side. I grip her hip, then slide my hand up her side, watching as the skin prickles in goose bumps. I swirl my fingertips around her breasts, flicking her hard nipples, which causes them to harden even more.

"Do you have condoms? I only had the one in my wallet."

"I think so," she says, "they'd be in the nightstand if I do."

We make out, enjoying the exploration of each other's bodies. I like finding what makes her body hum and fall apart for me. Thankfully she had some condoms, which we put to use, multiple times before the alarm on my phone blared way to early come morning.

I FINISH THE FINAL DRILL COACH HAS US RUNNING TODAY. AFTER the game yesterday and then the extra workout I got last night with Trinity, my body is screaming at me. I still wouldn't change one thing about the last twenty-four hours.

Good sex is like a drug, one hit and you are addicted. All I can think about is the next time I can slide into her. Take her hard and fast like she liked to best last night, or was that this morning? Our escapades are all morphing together.

"Damien, you doing okay?" one of the assistant coaches ask me as I skate some cool down laps at a slow pace. I'd kind of zoned out while skating them, so I didn't even see him standing on the bench watching me.

"All good, just a little sore," I tell him. "Nothing some time in an ice bath wont cure."

He nods his head in agreement, "All right. Just making sure. We're counting on you by time this season. We want to make it deep into the playoff and you're going to be a key piece of that happening."

"You know I'll do anything I physically can to make that a reality."

"That's what I like to hear. Now go get you that ice bath. I think after that, you're needed in the video room." I lift my chin, letting him know I heard what he said, then squirt a mouth full of water into my mouth. I gulp the cold liquid down until I empty the bottle.

"I didn't think we were reviewing tape today," I tell him as we both walk down the hall to the locker room.

"Not game tape, something about a promo video or something like that," he tells me. "I'm not sure the exact details."

The thought of a promo video makes me think of Trinity, and thinking of her makes my cock twitch in my jock, which isn't very comfortable at all. There isn't room in it for me to get hard. I push into the locker room, most of the other guys already out of their gear, some taking showers, some getting attended to by the medical staff, being stretched out, Ryker's submerged in one of the ice baths, which is where I'll be headed as soon as I get all my stuff stripped off.

I sink into the ice water, the coldness biting at my skin. It's not fun sinking into one of these, but the benefits are worth dealing with the few minutes of numbing pain. Once out, I head for the showers, letting the hot water also relax my muscles. "Fuck man, what attacked your back? Or should I ask who?" Tristan asks, a shit eating grin on his face. I continue to walk over to my stall, my towel wrapped around my waist.

"I don't kiss and tell," I retort.

"Looks like you had one hell of a night," he volleys back.

"It was all right," I give him a little tidbit.

"Damn man, I hope she sticks around then." I don't reply, just focus on pulling out my clean clothes and getting dressed. I pull on a pair of athletic shorts and a team t-shirt. I add a ball cap to my head and call it good.

I head for the video room. This is the place that we usually review game tape as a team, or sometimes one-on-one with a coach if they want to work on something specific with one player.

When I enter the room, I see a camera set up, facing a stool, which is across from another stool. Blake is currently on the stool being recorded, and Trinity is opposite of him, asking questions from a paper in her hand. I stay quiet, not wanting to interrupt the footage.

It doesn't take long before Blake is removing the microphone that was clipped to his shirt and handing it back. He slaps my hand, tugging me into a man hug-bump thing as he passes by me, then leaves the room.

"Hi," Trinity greets me after he's gone.

"Hi," I reply, my eyes roaming over her body. I lean down, bringing my lips to her ear. "It's so fucking hard not to kiss you right now."

I step back, but don't miss the way her breath catches from my words. The way her eyes flutter and the tongue peeking out to swipe at her lips proves just how much my words affect her.

"Where do you need me?" I ask, bringing her back to the present.

"The stool please, but first I need to attach this to your shirt," she says, holding up the small microphone.

She steps close, and as she touches my t-shirt, I grip her hip, giving it a good squeeze. "Dinner tonight?" I ask, my voice just above a whisper, but I know she can hear me seeing as how there's only a few inches between us.

"I'm supposed to have dinner with my best friend tonight, but you're welcome to join us." She says, then bites her bottom lip. "That is if you're not afraid to meet him this early in our relationship."

"Do you want me to meet him?" I ask.

"Of course, but I don't want to rush it if it's too early."

"When and where are we having dinner?" I ask. She smiles up at me, and I know I asked the right thing.

"Seven and at some new place he found that he wants to try. I can't remember the name of it right now."

"Want me to pick you up? We can take one car, maybe head back to my place afterwards?"

"I'd like that. Should I pack a bag to stay the night?"

"That's up to you," I give in slightly and kiss her cheek, right next to her ear. "I'll keep you busy in the sheets again tonight." She shivers at my words, the smoldering look in her eyes tells me all I need to know. "Tell me, Trinity, are your panties wet right now?"

She looks around, verifying that we are still very much alone in this room. "Maybe," she says coyly. "You'll have to wait until later to find out." She winks and walks over to the stool.

I take a seat on the stool that is open for me and slap my media face on. I might look a smidge less intimidating since the interviewer is much hotter to look at than the media I'm usually taking questions from.

"This is a little get to know you video. I'm going to ask you a list of twenty questions, don't over thing them. It's supposed to be fun."

"Okay," I agree, "Do you want me looking at you or directly into the camera?" I ask to make sure I'm doing as she needs.

"A mixture of both is okay," she says before pressing a button on a remote that is resting in her lap. "What is your go-to coffee order?" she asks first.

"Nitro brew with sweet cream."

"Favorite pre-game meal?" My eyes flick to hers and I can't help but smirk before answering.

"Chicken and shrimp pasta followed by a protein heavy smoothie."

"Favorite vacation spot?"

"That's a hard one. Greece is beautiful, but so is Scotland. I tend to spend most of my off time in Canada, but that's not really vacation," I ramble on.

Trinity goes down her list, one question at a time, all easy enough questions to give quick answers.

"All right, you're done. Thank you for helping me out by answering all of these."

"Anytime. When are you wrapping up here today?" I ask. I don't really know what her non-game day schedule is like, I guess I've never thought to ask, which makes me feel like a real asshole.

"I've got a couple more guys popping in today, then I'll be doing some editing. I'm not sure yet if I plan to do that here at the office or if I'm going to take it with me."

"What time do you want me to pick you up?" I ask.

"Oh, um, maybe around five?"

"Perfect, see you then." I set the microphone down on the table and flash her a wink before I exit the room.

I push the door open to the locker room. It is pretty empty as most guys have already left for the day. I gather my things and do the same.

Once home, I take care of a few things I need to get done. I strip my bed and toss the sheets into the washer. It's been a couple of weeks since I've done that, so it's time. I clean both the main bathroom off the hall and the master one. It's not that I don't keep a clean house, but it's also not every day that I have people over, specifically someone I'm dating. Just the thought of actually dating someone again is a strange concept.

Once the sheets are in the dryer, I start a load of clothes. We'll be going out of town again in a couple of days, so I need to make sure I have everything I need ready to go. This is our first long road trip, where we'll be gone ten days. They like to stack the entire east coast games together, which I don't mind. I figure get them over with when we can.

I haven't picked up groceries lately, so I start making a list of what I need at the store. Usually with a long road trip coming up, I'll do my best to eat up what I already have and just pick up takeout until after we get back. I started using a grocery service so that when I get home from longer trips, my fridge is already stocked. They bring it all in and put away what needs to be refrigerated or frozen. I just have to submit my list to them a day or so in advance and they get it taken care of. It might be a splurge to some people, but I find it helpful.

The dryer finally dings, so I pull the sheets out and get my bed re-made. I make sure to fluff all the pillows Kelly always insisted we have on the bed, making it look all nice and put together. I pick up the picture I have of the two of us. It was taken on our honeymoon. We were so young, happy, and in love. I have to wonder what life would be like had she not been killed that night. How many kids we'd have running around driving us crazy. "Love you, Kel," I say to the picture. "I hope you're proud of me. It took me a long time to be okay with moving on, but I think I've met someone you'd approve of."

My watch vibrates with a notification I've received a text message, so I set the picture back down on the nightstand and go in search of my phone so I can respond to the message.

TRINITY

Hey! I'm home and ready whenever you are.
:smily face:

I'll head that way shortly.

See you when you get here!

I smile at her enthusiasm. It is so different from my normal persona, but she's brought some much needed sunshine to my life. I guess they say that opposites attract, and there isn't much different than the broody old asshole of a guy and the cheerful, outgoing, too young for me woman falling for one another.

I take one more look around my place, making sure I didn't miss something that needs cleaned or put away. Confident my place is good enough to bring Trinity back to my place, I grab my keys and wallet and head out to the garage.

As I pull out of my neighborhood, I realize I'm getting kind of low on gas, so I pull into the next station and fill up.

I'm leaning against the side of the car while the tank is filling. "Excuse me," I hear. I turn to the voice and see a young kid, maybe ten, hell maybe thirteen years old standing there. "Are you Damien Thompson?" He asks. I notice right away the kid has on a Shockwaves hat and t-shirt.

"Sure am, you a hockey fan?" I ask him.

"Yes, sir," he says a little starstruck.

"What's your name?"

"James, James Hill." He holds out his hand and I shake it.

"Nice to meet you, James. Do you play?" I ask him. I notice a woman coming our way who looks a little frazzled.

"Just house league, but I hope to play travel one day."

"You any good?" I ask him, he looks a little on the small size, but that isn't a bad thing. Sometimes it's the little guys who can skate faster than anyone else.

He smiles wildly at me now but shrugs his shoulders. "I'm okay, nothing like you are."

I chuckle at that, obviously knowing that some kid isn't going to be at my level. "Want me to sign your hat?" I offer.

"I don't have a pen, but otherwise I'd day yes," he tells me just as the woman stops next to him.

"Sorry he was bothering you, he's such a people person," she says, obviously not having a clue who I am.

"Not a problem, ma'am. Do you have a pen in your purse I could use?" I ask her.

"Um, maybe," she says, and rummages around, pulling out a sharpie. "This is all I have, will it work?"

"Perfect," I tell her as I take it and then the hat from the kid and sign it.

"Who are you?" she finally asks, looking directly at me.

"Damien Thompson. I play for the Shockwaves. Is this your son?" I ask her.

She looks between the two of us, a little shocked herself. "Yes," she finally answers.

"You've got a good kid there, has your family ever been out to a game?"

"No, I can't really afford the tickets on a single mom salary," she says.

"I've been to a few of the practices. Those have been fun." James pipes up.

"Can you make it if I put some tickets out at will call for you, along with some food vouchers?" I offer.

"Mom, say yes, please say yes," James pleads with his mother.

"That's incredibly kind of you. I have no idea what game we could make it to with my schedule."

"How about this, I'll give you a number you can call or text after you've had the chance to look at the home schedule. Pick any game, and I'll make the arrangements for you to pick up everything at will call."

What's your work number? I need to give a kid a way to reach me for some tickets to a game.

The text bubbles pop up and I read the number Trinity texted me off to James and his mom.

"Hope to see you soon, have a good afternoon," I tell them both. I hand the sharpie back and turn back to my car, hanging up the gas nozzle.

"Mr. Thompson, do you mind if I take a quick picture with you?" James asks just before I slide into the driver seat.

"Sure kid," I tell him as I come back to stand behind my

car. I stand next to him while his mom snaps a quick picture.

"My teammates are going to be so jealous!" he exclaims as he steps away from me to look at the picture his mom took.

"Where do you play out of?" I ask.

"A rink down off of Mable," his mom answers.

"I can't say I've ever been there. Keep up the hustle and maybe I'll be seeing your name in the draft one day," I tell him before bidding them both goodbye.

I always enjoy making a kid's day when they recognize me when I'm out and about. I don't often offer up tickets, but something about this kid made me do it.

"So, what was up with the text?" Trinity asks when she gets into the car. She texted just before I pulled in that she was downstairs waiting for me, so I just pulled up along the curb when I got her.

I lean over the console, slip a hand behind her neck and pull her lips to mine. I keep the kiss quick as we're not really supposed to be parked where we are. I pull out and into traffic before we end up with someone mad at us.

"A young boy recognized me while I was pumping gas, and I signed his hat. He plays for a local house league, and after asking him if he's ever come to a game, his mom piped in that she's never been able to afford tickets on her single mom income. So, I asked if she'd bring him and offered to leave some tickets at will call," I explain.

"That's so kind of you, how does that work exactly? Do you have to go and actually buy them?" she asks.

I chuckle. "Not exactly, every player is allotted so many tickets. If they're married or have kids, they tend to use them. Sometimes they'll donate them for charity's to auction off, or donate them for first responders to attend, things like that. I told his mom to check the schedule and compare it to her work schedule, since that was something she was worried about, and then to call or text your number and we'd get things taken care of. I also offered to put some food vouchers with the tickets since I know the stadium food can be quite pricy."

"You're a good man, Damien," Trinity praises me.

"I'm still a broody asshole most of the time," I grunt.

"Not even close," she says as she runs her hand up and down my forearm. I grip her thigh with my large palm and can feel the heat building between her legs.

"Maybe not with you but ask any of the guys on the team and they'll tell you. I think I've earned a new badge too," I tell her.

"What's that?" She quirks a brow at me when I quickly glance her way. Traffic has come to a stop due to a red light up ahead.

"Cradle robber," I can't hold back the laugh that has built up thinking about that.

"Yeah, you kind of are," she agrees. "I never knew I'd like an older man, but damn, you've changed my mind."

"I'm not that old," I grumble.

"Should I start calling you *Daddy?*" she asks, practically purring the word daddy.

"Fuck no," I bark out.

"Okay, good. Because I don't think I could ever say it with a straight face or without giggling."

"You're trouble."

"But you love it," she quips.

I pull back into my place so we can drop off her bag and I can show her around before its time to head to dinner with her friends.

I lead her into my bedroom, and she drops the overnight bag on the end of the bed. "It's very masculine in here," she comments.

"Did you expect anything different?"

"No, not really. Although, the pillows are a nice touch."

"Kelly was big into pillows. I couldn't get rid of them after she died," I tell her honestly.

She notices the picture frame on the nightstand and walks around to that side of the bed. I watch as she picks it up and studies the picture. "She was so pretty, and holy shit, you look so young."

"That's because I was. And I have to agree, she was so beautiful, but she never let it get to her head. She was one of the kindest people I'd ever met in my life. I was lucky to have her for the amount of time I did."

She sets the photo back down, exactly how I had it and then walks over to stand in front of me. "I love that you've kept her memory alive in your home. So many people tuck away everything from their loved ones because it is hard to look at. I think it speaks volumes to how much you loved her that all these years later, she's still making an impact on your daily life. Don't ever change that."

I pull her into my arms and rest my chin on the top of her head. She's just shattered every fear I've had with starting a new relationship. I've always been worried that a new woman in my life wouldn't want me to have things from my marriage on display. Wouldn't want me to talk about her when I need to, but so far Trinity has welcomed all of that. "Thank you, she's still holds a part of my heart, and always will. I don't want you to feel like you're competing with her, but also know that I won't forget about her either."

"I wouldn't ever," she says then pushes up onto her toes and kisses me.

I pull her as tight as I can against me, deepening the kiss for a few minutes. Her cell phone dinging has us pulling apart, so she can check it.

"Time for us to go," she says, hitting a button to silence the phone. "I set an alarm so we wouldn't be late."

"Smart move." I chuckle. "Because I was about to take you to bed and ravish you, but I guess some actual food first is probably a good idea." I nip at her lips, then step back again and lead her out of the bedroom.

CHAPTER 16
TRINITY

I slip my hand into Damien's as we walk into the restaurant. The way people look at us, taking the two of us together in is something I've never experienced. Are they staring because they recognize him? Because of our obvious age difference? Whatever it is, I don't really care. What we have is between the two of us and that's all that matters.

We wait in the line to approach the hostess stand, "Did Michael tell you where they were seated?" Damien asks, his lips close enough to my ear that it sends shivers down my spine.

"No, just that they had a table," I tell him as we step forward.

"Good evening, do you have a reservation?" the older man asks.

"We're actually meeting friends here who have already been seated."

"Right this way," the man says as he escorts us to the table where Michael and Matteo sit. They've taken one side, leaving the other for us.

Both guys stand when we approach, Michael comes

around to pull me into a hug and whispers in my ear. "Damn girl, you did good. His pictures don't do him justice."

"Matteo, nice to meet you." The two men shake hands and it's almost like they have a silent conversation in that handshake.

"Likewise, I've heard a lot about the two of you," Damien tells the guys. He shakes hands with Michael before we all sit down.

"Hopefully it was only good things," Matteo jokes.

"Of course. Thanks for being such good friends to my girl here," Damien tells them as he places his hand on my thigh and squeezes it. I look his way, and he returns the look.

"Damn, he's good." Michael murmurs from across the table.

Our server approaches and takes everyone's drink orders. From the empty glasses on the table, I'm guessing the guys started before we got here, or maybe while they were waiting in the bar.

"What's it like to be a professional athlete?" Matteo asks.

Damien chuckles. "I don't really know how to answer that as it is all I've ever known as an adult, heck most of my childhood was also centered around hockey. Don't get me wrong, I love the game. I love the challenge of getting out there day after day, taking the beating to the body that it causes, but pushing through that to put everything in me to play to the best of my ability every single day. It doesn't always end how we want it, but it's still a fun way to make a living."

"Does the travel get tiring?" Michael asks.

"It can, especially when we get deep into the season. I haven't had anyone at home to worry about in a long time, but the guys who do, especially the ones with younger kids, it can start to wain on them and their spouses. We can be absent at times and that can be hard on relationships."

"So, it's a good thing then that Trinity will be traveling with you all the time then?" Michael asks.

He looks at me before answering, "I hadn't thought of that, but I guess you're right."

"The other guys are going to get jealous that your girl-friend is along on all trips," Matteo says.

"Nah, they're all good guys."

"You say that now, but when you guys are sexing it up in the hotel room, because let's face it, hotel sex just hits differently, they'll get jealous."

"We have our own rooms," I interject. "The players aren't allowed or aren't supposed to have women in their rooms overnight."

"There's always your room," Damien says and winks at me. I smack his biceps, my hand stinging from how hard his muscles are. "Don't hurt yourself." He laughs.

"Why do you have to be so hard?" I ask and realize my mistake as soon as the words slip from my lips.

"That's not usually what she says," Matteo murmurs and we all laugh, mostly at my expense.

The rest of the evening is filled with amazing conversation. By the end of the night, you'd never guess Damien had just met Matteo and Michael, which makes my heart so happy. I don't know what I'd do if they didn't get along. Matteo and Michael have been such important people in my life, I don't think I could be with someone that didn't like and get along with them.

"Thank you for tonight," I say once we're in the car. My heart and belly are both so full.

"I had a good time, thanks for inviting me." Damien lifts our clasped hands and kisses the back of my hand.

I watch as the skyline whips by as Damien drives us back to his place. My body is already humming with anticipation for later tonight.

Once inside, I take a seat on the couch. I'm not really tired, but also don't really know what the plan is for the rest of the night.

Damien joins me on the couch, sitting a little down from me. He lifts my feet and sets them into his lap, then starts massaging them. My head falls back on the cushion, the pressure in my arches feels so damn good.

"Do you know what time we're leaving on Tuesday?" I ask.

"Usually around nine, but an email is sent out about midday the day before with the full itinerary."

"Any tips for my first long trip?" I ask.

"Laundry services will be available along the way, so don't feel like you have to pack enough for the full ten days. Catering will be changed up, so it isn't the same thing every day. You already know the rinks can be cold, so you know how to dress in them. The weather outside shouldn't be all that bad yet, so you're probably find without winter clothes."

"I don't think I own true winter apparel."

"You'll want a heavier coat, good hat and gloves for when we visit some of the cities that experience cold, snowy winters."

"I hadn't really thought of that, guess I need to do some shopping."

"When we stop in Colorado, you should have some time to get to a store there. They have places like Columbia and The North Face which will both have good options for you."

"I'll keep that in mind and see if I can make it to one or both."

"What else do I need to know?"

"Ummm," he chuckles, "I don't really know. I've been doing this for so long that it is second nature to me. I guess making sure you have everything you need for your cameras and such, which I'm sure you'd do already. It isn't like we're in remote places. If you forget something you can replace it easily at any stop. One thing that might take a little getting used to is we often travel to the next city as soon as we finish up in one place. So, we'll be wheels up at eleven thirty, then fly to the next place and get to bed in the wee-hours of the morning. Usually when that happens, Coach gives us the morning off, unless it's the random time when we have to play back-to-back games."

"Okay, good to know. How does that work with the hotels? Don't you usually take afternoon naps?"

"They know we need late checkouts. I don't know the financial details on if they are charging the team for the night, but they allow us to check out when we leave for the rink, but that's taken care of by someone in the front office."

"Makes sense, but good to know that when we leave for the rink for the game, I need to be fully packed and ready to go. I'm guessing someone will tell me what to do with my luggage?"

"Yes, they come and collect it, then take it directly to the plane."

"Such a different way to travel. I'm not sure I'll be able to go back to commercial," I laugh.

"It is nice and makes you appreciate how well they move us from one place to the next."

"Are there any places you stay in the same place, but play multiple teams?"

"Yes, but not many. When we play New Jersey and New York, we actually stay in Jersey, just across the river from New York City. We move out to Long Island when we play them just because of the distance and how long it can take to get there driving."

"That makes sense. What about LA and Anaheim?"

"Because of traffic, we move hotels so we're close to the arenas. We can't risk being stuck in traffic."

"Got it."

"But, we also don't always necessarily play those two teams back-to-back. Since they are close to home, we sometimes just fly down in the morning and come back after the game. We'll have rooms for the daytime but won't stay overnight in them."

"So much for me to learn," I admit.

"You'll be a pro before you even realize it. Plus, the next road trip is only a couple games, so it will seem so much easier after doing a long one."

"I hadn't thought of that."

"Enough about work," Damien says. He grabs my hands and tugs me until I move and straddle his lap. "Much better," he says. "Now I can kiss you."

He just does that, kissing me gently at first, but quickly deepening the kiss as his hands roam around my body.

"Did I mention how much I love this top on you?" he asks as he traces the tops of my breasts that peek out the top.

"I don't think so," I tell him as I arch my back and press my chest out a little further for his appraisal.

"Every time I looked over at you during dinner, I'd get a hint at what you've got on underneath and it had me in a perpetual state of arousal."

"Mhmmm, sounds like a personal problem," I tease as he tugs my shirt down, taking the top of my bra cup with it. My hard nipple pops out and Damien lowers his mouth to it, flicking the hard bud, causing it to harden more.

I can feel his cock swell where our bodies touch. His hardness presses against my clit in the most delicious way.

"Yes," I moan.

"You like that, Sweetheart?" Damien says into my skin.

"Mhmmm," I whimper in agreement.

He tugs at the hem of my shirt, so I lift my hands up and allow him to pull it up and off my body. I'd usually feel so exposed, sitting in front of someone in just my bra, but the way Damien's eyes skate over my body with such lust has all those insecurities melting away.

"I could look at this view every day and never tire of it,"

he says before caressing both of my breasts. He slides a finger between my breasts and release the front clasp of my bra.

"I'm surprised you found that so quickly," I tell him as my bra joins my shirt on the couch next to us.

"This ain't my first rodeo, or front clasping bra." He smirks.

"Touché," I chuckle before kissing him. I run my hands through his hair, which I've realized he is a big fan of.

Damien stands up and I wrap my legs around his waist. "Time to move this to the bedroom," he says then carries me there.

He sets me down at the side of the bed. I'm feeling bold and feisty tonight, so I reach for the clasp on his pants and flip it open, then push them off his hips and down over his hard ass. Damien tugs at his shirt, removing it in a sexy move that leaves my mouth watering at the sight of his chiseled body.

I push his boxer briefs down, his cock springing free as the waistband passes by the hard shaft.

"You're a little over dressed, don't you think?" he asks.

I stand to my full height and unclasp the fly on my shorts, then shimmy out of them, taking my thong right along with them. No need to leave any article of clothing in the way.

"I had plans to remove that with my teeth," he rasps in my ear.

I attempt a sexy shrug, "Maybe next time," I tell him before I drop to my knees in front of him. I grip his cock, flicking my eyes up to his to watch him as he watches me. I swirl my tongue around his crown and love the moan it pulls from deep in his chest.

Damien gathers my hair together, holding it in his fist at the back of my head. I tease his crown, then slide my tongue along the underside of his shaft, all the way to the base, then back to his tip. "Fucking hell," he grits as my lips wrap around his crown and I suck, hard enough to hollow out my cheeks. I don't miss the tiny thrust he makes, probably out of pure loss of control.

I slide his cock in, as much as I can take until his tip is hitting the back of my throat. I slide it back out, then back in again, continuing this motion repeatedly as I drive him crazy and closer to his orgasm. While driving him crazy, I slide a hand down and circle my swollen clit, giving it some love as I suck him off.

"Sweetheart, you need to stop," Damien says, but I ignore him. I take his cock into the back of my throat and hum, the vibrations must send him over the edge. The first spurt of cum hits my throat and slides down. I pull him back some, but don't release the pressure I have as I suck him until he's done coming.

I release his cock with a pop, stoking his softening shaft as he falls back on the bed behind him. He pulls me up by my armpits, then kisses me hard. "That was intense, now how wet are you for me?" he asks as he slides me up his body. He pushes back, allowing his entire body to be splayed out on the bed, taking me with him.

He pushes me further up the bed, maneuvering me like its nothing. I've never been in this position, my pussy hovering over a man's face, but I forget all my worries the moment his mouth connects with my center. I'm already swollen, wet, and in need of an orgasm. Damien doesn't disappoint, he brings me to orgasm quickly. I slide over his stubble, which will probably leave my thighs with some beard burn tomorrow, but it will be worth it.

We lay next to one another, our heads on our own pillows as we face each other. We'd both have our hands on each other, not able to keep from touching one another.

"I want to take my time with you for the next round. Make you beg for it," Damien says as he caresses me.

"Yes, please," I agree. I'd probably agree to just about

anything right now with how I'm feeling after coming like I just did.

He rolls over to his nightstand and pulls out a box of condoms. The box is new, so he struggles for a second to get the box open, then pulls out a foil packet and rips it open. I watch as he rolls it down is length, his tip glistening as it's covered.

"On your back," he instructs, then slides between my legs. He presses a kiss just above my pubic bone, sliding his lips along my torso as he moves up. When our faces align, he kisses me, keeping it slow and languid. He pulls back and looks down, sliding the tip of his cock through my folds, hitting my clit a few times before he aligns hit tip with my opening and slowly sides in. His control is irritating as I instantly crave for him to be fully inside me. "Greedy, greedy." He chuckles as I attempt to push him in faster. "Just be patient, I promise I'll make it good for you."

With that, he lowers back down and kisses me once again. His tongue thrusting along mine at the same pace his cock thrusts inside my body. It's erotic and I find my orgasm building at a delicious rate.

Damien breaks the kiss, pushing up on one forearm as he reaches down and lifts one of my legs to hitch up over his hip. This allows him to thrust a little deeper, hitting me in just the right spot that my body hums with anticipation and need.

"You feel so good, dripping on my cock like that, Sweetheart." His pace picks up, a little more need building behind everyone. The room is filled with our mutual moans, and the sound of our bodies slapping against one another. "I'm so close," he tells me. I pull his lips to mine, but don't kiss him right away.

"Make me come," I plead then kiss him hard. He thrusts hard, his pubic bone grazing over my clit with each thrust. It only takes a few before I'm coming harder than I ever have.

"Yes," I cry out. "Please don't stop." I tell him and he doesn't, letting me ride out the best orgasm.

We both slow down, our bodies aligning perfectly. Its then realize my orgasm triggered his as well. "So fucking perfect," he kisses my shoulder, our bodies slick with sweat. He pulls in a few deep breaths before he rolls off of me, pulling me with him. He holds me in his arms, our bodies tucked against one another as we both bask in the orgasm hormones.

My body starts to chill as it cools down, so much that I shiver in Damien's arms. "How about a shower before bed?" he asks.

"Sounds perfect." I kiss his chest then push to sit up. I look at him over my shoulder. He's so relaxed and looks happy. I don't notice that broodiness I noticed the first time I met him, which really wasn't all that long ago when I really stop and think about things. Time really does fly by when you're having fun and living life to the fullest.

CHAPTER 17
DAMIEN
DECEMBER

"You can't be serious," I argue with Avery and Tori. "I can't be auctioned off anymore. I agreed to that before I was dating someone. This isn't fair to Trinity," I state.

"I thought the plan was for her to bid on you and win?" Avery replies.

"That was before we were dating. Now it just seems like a bad idea." I stand my ground.

"Sorry, the advertisements have been out for weeks that you're on the auction block. It will be fine; she can still bid on you and win. The charity will get a nice donation out of it."

"And why can't I just make a cash donation?"

"Because we have no idea how much money you'll bring in, plus the issue with the advertisements. You don't want us looking like idiots if we don't have you up there, do you."

I grumble, still not loving this idea, but I also don't want to make enemies with the WAG's. They could make my life miserable if they wanted.

"Fine, but I don't like it. This will be the one and only time I agree to this," I say, looking them both in the eyes so they know I'm serious.

"Of course. We wouldn't ask you to again," Tori says.

I leave the conference room the ladies were in, working on the charity event that is in a few days. I know they work hard on this every year, coming up with new themes and new ways to raise money. I don't fault them for sticking to our agreement, but I also don't have to be a fan of it.

I head down the hallway of the practice facility and run into Trinity on my way to the area we call the lounge. It's a large room, that is filled with comfortable seating, a large TV mounted on the wall, some games like pool, foosball, and ping pong are set up around the room. The entire back wall is a large kitchen where our nutrition services set up daily meals and snacks for us to have on hand. Anyone within the organization is welcome to come in here whenever they want something. We also have large refrigerators that are filled with lots of drink options to choose from.

"Hey," I greet Trinity. We've been able to keep out relationship on the down-low for the most part. I'm fairly confident almost everyone on the team knows, but they don't mention it, which I think Trinity appreciates. She doesn't want anyone to think differently of her just because we are together.

"Hi, how's your day going?" she asks. Today was an optional skate, which I didn't participate in. I came in to get stretched out and do some therapy with the trainers.

"Better now that you are here," I tell her as I quickly look around to see if anyone is around. When I know the coast is clear, I drop a quick kiss to her lips, but pull back just as quick. "I wasn't able to get out of the auction this weekend," I tell her.

"Did you think you would be able to?" She quirks a brow at me.

"Well, yeah, when I agreed to it, we weren't together."

"I'm not worried about it," She smiles up at me. "I mean, I have an unlimited budget to win you, right?" She flashes me a wicked grin, which only makes my cock swell.

"You're just as bad as Avery and Tori." I chuckle.

"I'll make it worth your while afterward," she says. "Unless you're going to insist on only a coffee date the next day with me." She knows damn well I won't.

"That's it, I'm booking us a room at the hotel. Expect to be dragged upstairs as soon as I come off that stage." I growl.

"Why Mr. Thompson, what kind of girl do you take me for?" she teases.

"Mine," I whisper into her ear. "All mine, and don't you forget that." I step back and see exactly what kind of effect my words have had. Her nipples are hard, pressing against the fabric of her bra and shirt. "Have you had lunch yet?" I ask, changing the subject.

"No, have you?"

"I haven't, but I was heading that way. Join me?" I ask.

"Sure," she agrees, and we walk to the lounge.

The smell of the grill top on hits me as we approach. I love the days that the chef is making food to order. When we walk in, they have the normal salad bar all set up, along with some grilled chicken breasts, and pasta salads set out. But the main focus today is the grill. There is a large spread of noodles, proteins, veggies and sauces you can compile to have the chef grill up into a bowl.

Trinity and I both grab bowls, filling them with everything we want. I grab a second one, filling it up just as full as the first. During the season, I have to keep my protein up, seeing as how many calories I burn each day during the season.

"Hungry today?" Trinity asks me as I hand over my bowls to the chef. He dumps them out on the large grill, adding some liquid to help them sizzle.

"I didn't get much protein with my breakfast," I murmur just above a whisper so only she can hear me.

Her cheeks turn red, as she turns to look at me. "Damien," she says my name behind gritted teeth, "Someone might hear you."

"And?" I ask, quirking a brow at her since she loves to do it to me.

She looks around the room, not a single person is paying attention to us as we stand here and wait for our food to be cooked. She turns back to me, rolling her eyes. "Nothing," she concedes.

"That's what I thought. You want me to make an announcement, because I will," I ask.

"No, but I'm sure they'll all figure it out come Saturday night."

"Does that bother you?"

She immediately shakes her head no. "I'm not ashamed of dating you, I just don't want anyone to get the wrong idea about my character. I didn't take this job to land a hockey player boyfriend."

"No one is going to think that. If anything, they'll thank you for putting up with my ass. I think you've softened my edges some."

"Speaking of Saturday, I need to go pick up my dress this week," she says. I sent her out shopping with Avery, Tori, and Kendra last weekend and told her to get whatever she wanted. Dress, shoes, lingerie. The works. I want her to feel spoiled and beautiful. She could wear a paper bag to the event, and I'd still think she was the most beautiful woman there, so I'm sure whatever she's picked will look great.

"I need to make sure you have a tie and pocket square that matches the red of my dress, if not, the store says they sell them in the matching fabric."

"Why don't you just buy what they have so we don't have to make a special trip back. Then we'll know for sure that everything matches perfectly," I suggest.

"Because you might have something already in your closet that works."

"Buy the tie and pocket square, Sweetheart. I don't care

about the cost." She nibbles on her bottom lip, as she mulls over what I've told her.

"Trinity, your order's up," Allen, the chef says as he holds up a plate over the protective shield they have between us and the grill.

Trinity takes her plate and sets it down at a table. I watch as she walks over to the counter that has silverware, napkins, and condiments on it. She grabs stuff for both of us, and returns to the table.

"Damien," Allen says, getting my attention. "Here's your lunch. She seems to be a good one," the older man says as me nods in Trinity's direction.

"She is, thanks man," I say as I take my heaping plate of food.

I sit down across from Trinity, not wanting to crowd her by taking the seat right next to her. However that backfires on me when Jason Soaps sits down right next to her. I know I don't really have to worry about him as he's happily married, but still that should be me next to her.

"What's up, Soapy?" I ask, using his nickname as usual. I don't think anyone on the team calls him Jason on a regular basis.

"Not a whole lot. What's up with the two of you?"

"Just grabbing some lunch."

"I met you wife the other day," Trinity pipes in. "She is so sweet. And I hear congratulations are in order."

"Yeah, we're pretty excited. A little shocked it happened so quickly, but here we are," he says.

He'd already shared the news in the locker room earlier this week, so I'd congratulated him then.

"She was very excited when she spilled the news at lunch to all the girls." I guess she met up with the other ladies when they went dress shopping for next weekend.

"Now that she's out of here first trimester, she's been feeling better. Her belly kind of just popped out in the last few days it seems. Now I just can't wait to feel the baby kick, but she says that will be a few more weeks."

"Aww, poor girl. I'm sorry she had a rough time during the first trimester," Trinity tells him.

"It wasn't as bad as it could have been, but she definitely had a handful of bad days."

I dig into my food, the flavors all coming together so perfectly. I demolish everything on the plate, and wish I'd had more since it was so good.

"You heading home or sticking around?" I ask Soupy once I'm done eating.

"I've still got to meet with Trinity here for my question session." I kind of forgot about that. She's been spreading those out a few at a time and releasing them one a week for the fans. It's been a huge hit. She told me all about how her boss gave her a raving review due to how she's been managing the team's social media and connecting with fans.

"Oh, before I forget," she says and turns to face me. "I got a call this morning from that Cassidy. She's the mother of that boy you promised tickets to a while back."

I perk up at that, I'd kind of forgotten about them. "What did she say?" I ask.

"She picked a game over James's Christmas break. She said she gets some extra time off then as well since he's out of school."

"I'll get the vouchers ready and leave them with the office."

"Who's this?" Soupy asks.

"A kid that recognized me at the gas station a while ago. Plays at a rink here in town. I asked him and his mom if they'd ever made it out, but she said she'd never been able to afford to get tickets to bring him, so I invited them to a game." I tell him. We've all done things like this, so it really isn't a big deal.

"Since it sounds like time won't be an issue that day, you

should talk to Coach about inviting him out for morning skate. Give him the ultimate experience."

"That's not a bad idea." I tell him.

Coach walks into the lounge right then, "Coach," Soupy calls out, getting his attention and waving him over.

"These guys giving you a hard time?" Coach asks Trinity when he approaches.

"No, not at all," Trinity tells him and it takes everything in me not to lean over and whisper that's not what she would have said this morning in the shower, but I keep those thoughts to myself. Thankfully I've perfected my poker face and don't even give away my dirty thoughts on my face.

"Damien's giving a young kid tickets to a game, I suggested he get permission to invite him to morning skate that day, give him the real experience," Soupy tells him.

"I don't see a problem with it," Coach says as he places his hand on my shoulder and squeezes. "I'm sure it would make his day."

"He said just the picture and autograph I gave him was going to make his team jealous, so I can only imagine what this would do. He'll be the most popular kid in his league."

"Has the team ever gone out and done outreach with some of these house leagues?" Trinity asks. "That would be a marketing jackpot," she says.

"We haven't, but it is definitely something we could look into. I know the team has handed out some grants for equipment and offsetting the cost of ice time, but we've never sent players out to do anything."

"Some free clinics would also be an idea," Trinity says. "And might be easier to schedule as you could have them here."

"You work with the front office and send me a proposal of how much time you need from the players, and we'll make it happen. Giving back is an important part of being in the community," he tells her.

"Looks like you've got your work cut out for you," I tell her.

"I don't mind. I'll call Cassidy back and make sure that will work out for them. Then I'll get to work on some community outreach. I bet she can give me the contact info for James's league, and I can start with them."

"That's a great idea. Talk to Nathan about inviting these kids leagues to come out to a game as a team. If I had to bet anything, he'd offer up a suite to a team or at least a block of tickets."

"I love it!" Trinity exclaims. "Thanks for having lunch with me, but I've got some work to get done."

"See you later," I call out as she steps away. The smile she flashes when she looks back tells me she got my double meaning. To everyone else in the room, it was just polite, but she knows that I mean I'll see her this evening. Preferably naked and underneath me in bed.

CHAPTER 18

TRINITY

I turn from side to side, getting a look at myself from all angles. The dress that I picked out is the fanciest thing I've ever purchased. As soon as I slipped it on in the dressing room, I knew that it was the one. That was solidified as soon as I walked out of the dressing room and all the ladies gushed over it, and insisted I buy it.

"Fuck," Damien growls from the doorway. He leans on the jam, his eyes raking from the top of my head where my hair is pulled up into a fancy updo, all the way down to my bare feet. The heals I bought to go with the dress aren't the most comfortable things, but they are the perfect touch to complete the outfit. "You're a smoke show and every guy in that room is going to have his eyes on you."

"But yours are the only ones I care about," I tell him. I take in the suit he's got on. It was tailored perfectly for his muscular frame and has my body humming with desire.

"Damn straight." He closes the distance between us, then tugs me the last inch or so that was between our bodies. "If we didn't have a car showing up in ten minutes to pick us up, and you hadn't just spent the last few hours at the salon, I'd rip this dress off of you and fuck you right here, bent over the counter."

"You're incorrigible sometimes, but I wouldn't have you any other way." I kiss him quickly as I don't want to mess up my makeup.

"Only for you, Sweetheart."

"How about we do all that, plus some tonight in the hotel room," I suggest. The way his eyes darken with lust tells me he likes that idea.

"I'll hold you to that." He smirks at me.

He lets me go and I leave the bathroom, gathering my shoes, overnight bag, small purse, and phone. The bellman will take our bags to the room for us when we arrive, that way we can go directly into the ball room and tonight's festivities.

"I don't care what the bids get up to, make sure you're the winner," Damien reminds me in the car.

"What kind of dollar amount do you think it will get to?" I ask. I guess I hadn't really though much about it, but in the back of my mind I was thinking it would be only a few thousand.

"Probably fifty thousand," he says, nonchalant and my jaw drops.

"Are you serious?" I ask.

"Yes, Sweetheart. People with money to burn come to these events. They don't often hold back if there is something on the docket they want. I've seen people pay twice what something is worth, just to say they won it and the money went to a good cause. There will be lots of alcohol flowing at this event as well, which helps loosen up peoples' wallets."

"That's crazy. And you're okay with spending that kind of money, basically on yourself?"

"I look at it as I'm making sure I only have to go on a date with you and not some prissy woman who thinks that I'll forgo the coffee date and fall madly in love with her."

"That was oddly specific." I laugh.

"It happened to a buddy of mine years ago," he says and my eyes go wide. "He had to get a restraining order to get this chick to leave him alone. It was crazy. Thankfully once he did that, she backed off and left him alone, but it was sketchy until then."

"Wow, okay then. I'll make sure to win."

"Good girl." He whispers into my ear, "I'll reward you accordingly later tonight."

The car pulls up to a red carpet. One side is lined with so many cameras and reports, I'm a little overwhelmed as we step out of the car. Damien steps out first, then turns to offer me his hand. I take a deep breath before I place my feet on the ground and stand up. My heels give me some extra height, but he still towers over me. I slip my hand into the crook of his arm as we walk down the carpet. We stop in the center, allowing for our picture to be taken turning in each direction for a few minutes before we're shown down the line and into the hotel.

"I think I'll be blind for the next ten minutes after that," Damien says.

"Same," I tell him as we make our way inside. I find our names on the seating map that is displayed next to the doors. We make our way into the room, Damien gets stopped by a few different people, each time he makes sure to introduce me to them.

"Do you want something from the bar?" he asks motioning to one of the many that are set up.

"Sure," I reply, and we walk up to one with the shortest line.

"I'll take whatever blonde you've got on tap," he tells the bartender, "and whatever she'd like."

"I'll take the Blue Breeze," I tell her after reading the different cocktail specials they have printed on a large sign.

"Of curse, your total is eighteen dollars," she tells Damien.

He holds up his credit card to the reader, paying for our drinks while the bartender finishes making mine. She passes the two glasses across to us, and one sip of my drink and I know it will be dangerous. Its fruity enough that I can't even taste the alcohol.

"Good?" Damien asks after he takes a drink from his beer.

"So good, and dangerous," I explain, telling him about the fruitiness of it.

"Have as many as you want," he gives me a devilish grin, "I can only imagine how fun you'd be drunk."

"I don't want to embarrass myself," I tell him.

"I won't let you do that, but letting go a little wouldn't be a bad thing."

"We'll see. I have to stay sober enough to win my date with you." I wink at him.

"Damn straight."

We walk from the bar to our table, where we're seated with Ryker and Avery, Aiden and Tori, Tristan and Kendra, and Blake, who apparently didn't bring a date with him.

Blake whistles when we approach, "Damn man, when did this happen?" he asks, circling his finger between Damien and me.

"Where have you been? This has been going on since the season started," Tristan pipes up.

"Guess I really have had my head in the game." He chuckles.

"Good for you, if he treats you badly, you know where to find me." Blake winks and Damien reaches out and smacks the back of his head.

"Asshole," Damien grunts.

"I'm just giving you shit; I can't believe it finally happened. Someone pulled you out of your shell long enough to realize you aren't an asshole all the time," Blake says.

"Something like that," Damien says.

"I don't know what you guys are talking about, Damien has never been like that since I've known him," I say.

"Interesting," Blake singsongs. "So, you pursued her then." He says, more so as a statement than a question.

"Good evening." A voice comes over the sound system and everyone in the room quiets down. "Thank you all for joining us tonight as we raise money for a worthy cause. Please be ready to open those checkbooks as you eat, drink, and buy the amazing items we have for you tonight," Nathan Bailey says and the room erupts in laughter.

"Before dinner is served, I'd first like to thank all the many volunteers who have made tonight happen. From the foundation staff to the wife group of our players. This night wouldn't have happened if it wasn't for all of them," he says, and the room erupts into a round of applause.

"Once dinner is finished, we'll be back with the live auction," Nathan says before stepping away from the podium. The servers all start bustling out from the back, bringing large trays with appetizers for each table. When tickets were sold, each attendee had to submit their dinner selection, so as long as things are running smoothly, the servers already know what to bring to each table.

"Thank you," I tell the young woman who sets down the plate with shrimp cocktail in front of me.

"Of course, ma'am," she says before moving to my left, serving Blake and making her way around, seat by seat.

Everyone digs into their food, along with the bread baskets that were brought to the table. Conversation flows easily between everyone. The more time I spend with everyone at this table, the more it feels like I'm building friendships and not just colleagues.

"Trinity, do you travel to every away game with the team, or do you get to stay back ever?" Tori asks.

"I travel to all of them," I tell her. "I'm sure if I requested a trip off, they'd allow it, but they like that road coverage to keep connected with the fans back home," I explain.

"That makes sense. I was just hoping to be able to invite you to our watch party we have when the guys are gone."

"Oh, that's so sweet of you," I tell her.

"When are you ladies planning on a trip with the team?" Tristan asks.

"January, when you guys are down in Florida," Avery says.

"Smart," Ryker chuckles.

"Come on, you don't want to visit Toronto or Edmonton in February?" Aiden asks.

"Not no, but hell no. I don't like the cold," Avery says.

"Do all the wives come on this trip?" I ask.

"And girlfriends!" Kendra adds. "Hopefully we can plan some things that you can sneak away and join us for."

"I'd love that, and one of the benefits of my position is I can mix up what kind of footage I take for each game. So as long as I'm there for the actual game, I can be flexible."

"Perfect!" Tori says.

"I just had an idea!" I say, ways I can pull this off already flying through my mind. "If it's okay with everyone on the trip, I can get some footage and give another look to what it's like for the families of the players. What its like for the guys to have their wives or girlfriend at an away game."

"Ohh, I love it. You could also do something similar when they have the moms' trip and dads' trip."

"When is that?" I ask.

"It is two separate trips. Usually when we have a two-game road trip. They take moms, or important women in our lives, so it can be an aunt or sister if our moms can't make it, for example," Ryker explains. "The dads' trip is the same. Some guys have an uncle, brother, maybe an old coach who made a big impact in their life if their dad can't attend."

"I love that!"

"The trips are usually a big hit. They travel with us on the team jet, stay at the same hotel. We take them out and go golfing or whatever is organized for the trip based on what cities we're visiting."

"I hope you all enjoyed your dinner," Nathan comes back over the sound system. "The live auction will start in five minutes, so if everyone involved would please head backstage, we'd appreciate it.," he instructs.

"Guess that's me," Damien grumbles.

"Make us proud," Aiden calls out at him. Damien flips him the bird as he walks away, and all the guys bust up laughing.

"Good evening," a man up on stage says. "I'm Bruce, and I'll be running this live auction tonight. If you check the pocket hanging on the back of your seats, you should find a bidder paddle, please pull those out now and we'll get this party started!"

We all pull out our paddles, ready to bid on some items.

"First up, we have a round of golf for four people, with carts at The County Club Resort and Spa. Valued at one-thousand dollars. Let's open it up at five hundred," he calls out, quickly increasing the bid until it finally closes at a whopping four-thousand dollars.

After the first four auction items go for well over their value, it is apparent that Bruce has a way with people and making them spend their money on these items.

"Next up, we have a one-of-a-kind item. A coffee date with none other than Damien Thompson from the Shockwave.!" Bruce calls out as Damien saunters out onto the stage with him. All the guys at our table let out some wolf whistles as they hoot and haller at Damien. "Looks like you've got yourself a fan club," Bruce chuckles into the microphone. Damien laughs but shakes his head at the ruckus the guys are making.

"Are you ready to get that paddle going?" Tori asks. "Or

are you going to make him sweat it out and not bid until the final call?"

"I hadn't thought of my strategy. I'm so nervous that I'm going to mess up," I tell them.

"Don't worry, we've got your back," Avery states.

"Good, because Damien warned me this might get up there in price and I don't know if I can stomach spending that much money."

"Pfft," Ryker says, "Spend Damien's money, someone ought to do it."

"All right, lets get the bidding started at five-thousand," Bruce calls it and at least fifteen paddles fly up in the air. He chuckles. "I guess you're a popular guy." He looks at Damien who just shrugs.

"Ten-thousand!" a woman stands up and yells out.

"Twelve-thousand!" and other one yells. My heart is pounding hard in my chest, and I'm frozen in place.

"Fifteen-thousand!" Avery yells, holding up my paddle.

Bruce's head bounces from one direction to the next as the bids are being yelled out for him.

"We've got fifteen, can get twenty?" he asks the room and five more paddles go up. "Twenty-five," he calls out and the same five paddles stay up in the air. "Now give me thirty-five," he says and two of them lower back down.

My heart rate slows down ever so slightly. "Okay, I've got thirty-five, now let me hear forty-thousand," he calls out, one of the women whose paddle has gone up every time stands up and yells out.

"Forty-eight thousand."

I don't know where I find the courage, but I grab my paddle and stand up. "Fifty-two thousand."

"Fifty-five," the other woman calls out immediately.

"Sixty!" I find myself yelling. Damien flashes a smile my way.

"We've got sixty on the table. Going one, twice, sold to the lady in the back. Paddle number 102," he calls out and everyone claps. I collapse back into my seat, shell shocked that I just spent sixty thousand dollars of Damien's money in the matter of a few minutes.

"Good job," Avery tells me as Bruce announces the next item up for bid. This one is for a ten-day trip in Sweden, which sounds amazing when he outlines all the details of said trip. I can only dream about something like that. It quickly gains large bids and ends up selling for more than one-hundred thousand dollars.

Damien finally makes his way back to the table, two drinks in his hands as he sits back down. A beer for himself and another Blue Breeze for me. "Thank you," I tell him as I take the drink from his hand.

"You did good," he leans in to tell me.

"I froze at first," I admit.

Damien chuckles. "Is that why Avery bid first?"

"Yes," I admit.

"We wouldn't have let her fail you," Ryker tells him. "I was ready to stand up and yell out one-hundred grand, but didn't want to upstage your girl."

"I would have made you pay that bid. I only agreed to cover Trinity's bid," he smarts back.

"Yeah yeah, you just aren't my type, even if it is just for coffee," Ryker jokes back. "But something tells me the two of you won't be going for just coffee."

"Oh, I'm getting my coffee date out of this," I state and the entire table erupts in laughter.

We visit while the remainder of the auction takes place.

"Do you want to go check out the silent auction items?" Damien leans over and asks after while.

"Yes," I tell him. He stands up, then offers his hand to me. I slip mine into his, and he tugs to to a stand.

"Have I told you lately how beautiful you are tonight?" he asks, his lips next to my ear.

"Just a few times." I smile up at him. He drops his lips to mine and gives me a quick kiss.

"Get a room," Blake calls out, which makes me laugh against Damien's lips.

"We've got one, its right up stairs," Damien retorts.

I slip my hand into his, linking our fingers as we walk to the other side of the room where the tables are set up. We look at all the different items, stopping to read a few of the tags. "See anything you want?" Damien asks.

"Oh, I don't know. I've already bought the best auction item here tonight," I tell him cheekily.

Damien stops walking and tugs me until we're facing each other. "Bid on whatever you want, I don't care what it is or the cost. I'll buy it for you."

"I don't need you to buy an overpriced auction item," I tell him.

"I know I don't need to, but what if I want to?" he asks.

"I don't know." I admit.

"I want to spoil you, I have the means to do so, so let me," he says.

With that, how can I tell the man no? I pull him back to looking at all the items. I find a private cooking class for two with a local chef. I think that could be a pretty fun date, so I tell him to bid on that. He does so, as well as for a few jewelry pieces that I really liked.

CHAPTER 19
DAMIEN

THE NIGHT HAS FINALLY WOUND DOWN ENOUGH THAT WE CAN escape without it being a big deal. I'm pretty sure my bids on the few silent items that Trinity liked will be winners. I made sure to bid generously on them. She might not want me spending money on her, but I *want* to spoil her. If anything, I can use the excuse that Christmas is just around the corner and give them to her as gifts.

"Did you enjoy yourself tonight?" I ask as I pull her close in the elevator. We're the only ones in here now that we've stopped on one other floor to drop off another couple.

"I did. I'm glad we came," she says as she lays her head on my chest.

"That's not the only coming you'll be doing tonight," I say and she just chuckles.

"I walked right into that one," she says as she continues to laugh.

"But it was a good one, you have to give me that."

"Maybe," she says as she looks up. Looking down at her I see so much in her eyes. It's on the tip of my tongue to tell her just what she means to me, but I can't get the words out. I can't tell her I love her yet. It hasn't been long enough for love to be in the picture, has it? Is there a minimum amount of time before you can fall in love with someone. Lust, I don't think so, but true love?

The elevator dings and the doors slide open. We walk out and down the hall to the suite I reserved. I picked up the keys when I drove down here this afternoon and checked in for the night. I open the door and see our bags sitting just inside the room where the bellman assured me we'd find them.

"Wow, look at this view." Trinity gasps as she looks out the window. She kicks off her heels before walking over to look out. It shows off the skyline and water. The Golden Gate Bridge is all lit up in the distance.

"I'd have to agree, the view is spectacular." I say, but my eyes are only on her standing in the window. I walk up behind her and press my lips to her exposed neck. I've craved kissing her in that exact spot all night. All that skin on display has been driving me crazy. "I could fuck you right here against the windows," I say as I nip at her ear.

"Mhmm, that's an interesting idea," she says and presses her ass back and against my growing cock.

"Can I take this dress off of you now?" I plead.

She turns in my arms, linking hers over my shoulders and behind my neck. "Absolutely," she says before I kiss her tenderly. I take my time, kissing and nipping. I find the side zipper, tugging it down to her hip. The dress falls from her body, pooling at our feet. I get my first view of the undergarments she's got on and had I know *this* is what she was wearing, we would have been up in this hotel room hours ago.

"Fuck, you're a sight, and a masterpiece."

"You like?" she asks coyly.

"Such a little vixen," I growl as I run a fingertip along the see-through material that's acting like a bra and thong. I tuck a finger under the thin strap that's stretched along her hip, quickly gripping it and pulling hard until the fabric loosens and rips right off her body. The gasp from her lips tells me she didn't expect that little move.

I fall to my knees and drop a kiss to just above her mound and slide my fingers into her folds. I find them wet and ready for me, just the way I like it. "You good, or do we need to find somewhere with more support for you?"

"If you plan to use that tongue on me, I'll need some support if you don't want me falling over," she says. I back her up against the full window, the lights of the city lighting her up from behind.

With the window supporting her, I hook a leg over my shoulder and latch onto her clit.

"Fuck, Damien," she cries out and it is the most beautiful sound. Her nails scratch against my scalp and I know I've got her exactly where I want her. Needy and ready to come apart.

I flick and suck, side my fingers in and out as I build her orgasm up, then back off, not allowing her to come, knowing that when I do it will be explosive. I blow on her clit, and she shudders. "I need to come," she cries.

"Soon, Sweetheart," I look up and tell her. The desire shining back at me tells me she's ready. I suck her clit back into my mouth as I sink three fingers inside. I press up until I find the rough patch on the inside and rub circles on it as I play her clit until she's throbbing and falling over the edge. Just like I knew she would, her explosion is epic. Her body goes rigid so much so that I can't move my hand for a few seconds. Once she relaxes and starts to slide down the window, I back off and swoop her up into my arms and carry her over to the bed.

As Trinity lays on the bed, basking in her orgasm, I shut my suit off, laying it over one of the chairs. I grab our bags and bring them over by the bed. I unzip mine to grab the box of condoms when I realize I forgot them on my bed. I took them out, but fucking forgot to pack them with us.

"Fuck," I mutter.

"What's wrong?" Trinity asks as she sits up on the bed. Her tits look so good, still cupped in that bra like they're on display for me.

"I forgot the condoms," I tell her.

"Oh, I'm on the pill, so I'm good if we want to forgo them."

I quickly walk back over to the bed, sitting down next to her. "Are you sure. I can run to the store and get some more, or we can just get creative. I don't want to pressure you into anything you aren't ready for."

She stands up off the bed and pushes her way between my thighs as I sit on the edge of the bed. My eyes are right at her breast height with how we're positioned, so don't miss the opportunity to press a kiss right between them.

"My eyes are up here." She tips my head up and I flash her a devilish grin.

"I'm aware, but your perfect tits are right here," I lower my head and lick at her nipples quickly before looking back up at her.

"I wouldn't have offered to go without them if I wasn't okay with it. I know I'm clean and I'm pretty confident you are as well. And well, if something was to fail, I don't think I'd be ad about it."

My heart rate increases as the blood starts to whoosh in my ears. "You're sure?" I ask again.

"Screw it," she mutters, "Damien, I've fallen in love with you. I know this might be too soon, and that might scare the shit out of you, but I can't not tell you how I really feel." She pauses to suck in a deep breath and blow it back out again.

I run my hands down her body, locking my arms around by her so she's trapped in my embrace.

"Say it again." I smile wide as I look up into her eyes.

She looks a little confused as she's just said a lot, but I just want to hear those three little words again. "I love you?" she says, but it comes out more as a question than a statement.

"Well, that's really fucking perfect, because I love you too." I seal my statement with a searing kiss. Pulling her into my lap and devour her.

I slide her off of my lap, only so I can lift my ass off the bed and remove my boxer briefs. I stroke my cock a few times, and have to remind myself not to bust a nut as soon as I slide into her without a condom. It has been years since I've had sex without one, so I'm sure it will feel like it's my first time all over again.

"How do you want me?" Trinity asks as we lay facing one another. Shes trailing her hands up and down my body, my muscles jumping to attention with every swipe of her skin.

"I'm not picky," I tell her.

"Either am I, she says as she rolls onto her back and takes me with her. I hook a leg over my hip, opening her up so I can get deep. I let the tip of my cock slide through her folds, getting it wet with her juices.

"Please," she cries as I tap against her clit. "I need you inside me."

I align my cock with her entrance and thrust home. I slide in until I'm balls deep. The way her body grips around my cock has me seeing stars already.

"Fuck," I yell. "Your pussy feels so good wrapped around my cock," I whisper into her ear as I start thrusting at a wild pace. I know she comes hard when I fuck her hard, so I'm not about to not give her what she wants.

CHAPTER 20
TRINITY

"MAY I PLEASE SPEAK WITH CASSIDY?" I ask.

"This is Cassidy."

"Hi Cassidy, this is Trinity Black with the San Francisco Shockwaves. We spoke the other day regarding the game you can make it to that Damien Thompson would like to invite you and your son to."

"Oh, yes, thank you for calling me back."

"Of course, I've got ticket vouchers, food vouchers, and a parking pass here for you. Damien would also like to extend one other invitation to you and James," I start to explain.

"Wow, I still can't believe he's just giving us all of this," she says, shock evident in her voice.

"Well, it gets better," I say. "The team would like for James to come hang out for the day with them. Show up to the game-day skate, have lunch with them, then come back when they arrive pre-game to let him experience what the guys do each game day. Both of you will get to watch warmups from the players bench, and then James will get to be dressed out on the ice for the National Anthem."

"Are you serious?" She almost screams in my ear. I can hear her sobbing through the phone at what I've just told her.

"I am, ma'am. Will being with the team most of the day work with your schedule?"

"Yes, I'm off that entire day. Thank you so much. I don't even know what to say. James is going to be so shocked and excited."

"I bet he is. Would it work for you to pick everything up from our office? I can meet you and show you exactly where to come on that day. If you're able to pick it up before Christmas, maybe you can wrap it up as a gift?" I suggest.

"You're a genius!" she exclaims. "This year has been really tough. My husband passed away last year and it's been a really hard time. I wasn't sure I was going to have much for James under the tree, but I was making do with what I could afford or quality for."

"I'm so sorry to hear that, I hope that we can bring a little good to both of your lives," I tell her and mean it.

"I don't have to work until around noon tomorrow, can I stop by around eleven?" she asks.

"That's perfect. Do you know where our practice facility is located?"

"I do, we've been there once for one of James hockey games."

"Perfect. That reminds me, do you happen to have the contact information for the league coordinator James plays in or at least the name of the league?"

"He plays for the San Francisco youth hockey association, I don't have their contact info handy, but I know they have a website that has it all." She says.

"Perfect, I've got it loading now and it looks like they have an email to contact, so I'll reach out to them that way. We want to possibly offer some free camps for kids occasionally and figured partnering with a youth organization was the best place to start."

"I'm sure they would love that! " she says. "Camps are so costly due to the ice time, it makes it hard to get him signed up. Some will offer scholarships, but not all of them do." She explains.

A few ideas are already forming. James can't be the only kid from a family that struggles to pay for him to play, so I wonder what we can do about that.

"Thank you for all the information, I'll see you tomorrow around eleven," I confirm before we end the call.

I get up and head out of my office. I'm on a mission and head straight for the executives offices, hoping to find Nathan in the office today.

I stop at Rose's desk, she's Nathan's personal assistant and such a sweet woman. "Hey honey, what can I do for you?" she asks as I approach.

"Is Nathan in today? I had a big idea that I'd like to run by him, but it is time sensitive," I explain.

"He is, let me check if he's busy. He just got off a confer-ence call," she tells me as she picks up her phone receiver and presses a button in it.

"Nathan, do you have a few minutes for Trinity? She'd like to speak to you if possible." She tells him. "Of course," she says and sets the phone back down.

"He's available, head on in," she says, pointing to his closed office door.

I push the door open and find Nathan standing to greet me. He rounds his big desk and motions for me to take a seat on one of the comfy chairs he has in the center of his office. Two large chairs face a short couch, about the size of a love seat. He sits across from me, giving me the floor to speak.

"What do you got for me?" he asks.

I explain the situation with James and how he met Damien, and now will be coming to the game, as well as everything before the game. I also explain the camp sugges-tion that I want to look into, but what I really came to ask him something even bigger.

"What do you think of starting a scholarship. I've thought

of a few ways it could work. One, we take applications, and a committee would review each application. We could offer different levels of scholarships, from full ones that include everything from their registration fees, to gear. To partial scholarships that maybe only cover registration or gear. The other idea would be to sponsor the entire league, but that might become a little costly."

"You have some good ideas, Ms. Black. I do like the first option. I think we could help more kids if we're only helping those that can't afford it. I could probably get some other business in the area to kick in some funding so we could reach even more kids."

"I love that. Do you think the program could extend to cover kids who want to play travel or higher levels, but can't afford to?" I ask, thinking specifically of James.

"I'm sure we could figure out a way to offer scholarships for those kids as well."

"That's so amazing, if theres anything I can do to help make this happen, I'm happy to help. Even if I need to donate some time outside of work for it."

"I appreciate that but let's not worry about that part of it yet. I did want to ask about something you said about James and his mother," Nathan says. "You said she's coming tomorrow to pick up stuff from you, is that correct?"

"Yes, on her way to work, she's going to stop by."

"All right, we might need to work fast then, but I think we can accomplish it. I'll have Rose help you if needed," he says. "I want you to go to go out and buy some gifts. Gift certificates to clothing stores, grocery stores, gas stations, those prepaid Visa cards, make sure some are to stores for the mom, not just for her son. Get five-thousand dollars' worth from various places. I'm going to call down to the equipment guys and have them put together a hockey bag filled with accessories. Pucks, tape, skate guards, training items, etc., then I want you to go into the team store and grab a few t-shirts, sweatshirts, a hat, whatever you think the kid might like and wrap everything up. We're going to make their Christmas magical."

The generosity of this man is astounding. I have tears of my own running down my face at how much this will mean to Cassidy.

"That is so nice of you," I tell him.

"Why have wealth if you don't help those in need," he says like it's nothing. "Rose has a company credit card she can give you to use, but also has access to petty cash if you have any issues with buying the gift cards on a credit card."

"I'll check in with her then. By the way, how's the baby and Harper doing?" I ask.

"They are both doing wonderful. We named her after my grandmother, Betsy whose actual name is Beatrice. It made my grandmother's day. But we've taken to calling the baby Bea," he says, and his face just lights up as he talks about his daughter.

"Aww, I bet she just loved that, and what a sweet thing for them to share."

"We're taking Bea back to Tennessee for the holidays, our families are over the moon excited to meet her."

"I bet. Are your moms still both here?" I ask.

"They are. Its going to be a feat to convince them to stay home when we're ready to come back." He chuckles.

"That first grand baby is quite alluring, I'm sure."

"Something like that," he says. "I don't want to seem rude, but I've got another phone call happening in a few minutes."

"Thank you for your time. I'll get right on our special project. Will you be around tomorrow to help deliver the surprise?" I ask.

"I don't believe so, but let Cassidy know that it is from all of us," he says.

"Will do, thank you, Nathan." I shake his hand and he

follows me out the door. We stop at Rose's desk, and he gives her the run down of what he told me. She immediately pulls a credit card out of a lock box in her desk and hands it over to me.

"I'll leave you two ladies to it," Nathan says before stepping away and down the hall.

"If you can give me twenty minutes, I can wrap up what I'm working on and then we head out together. I have an idea of the perfect place to go to first."

That sounds great," I tell her. "That will give me time to go save what I was working on and shut down. I have a feeling this is going to take us the rest of today."

"I think you're right," she says.

I look around the conference room and it looks like a wrapping booth exploded in here. We've got paper scraps all around us, gift bags galore, and a big pile of beautifully wrapped gifts. We ended up just putting a large bow on the hockey bag as it was too hard to wrap it without a box. I hope that Cassidy's car will be big enough to fit all of this into it. Rose had the idea of wrapping each gift card in a box. The team store had tons of size options in the recycle, so we had fun picking through them to find what we needed.

"I can't wait to see her face tomorrow," I tell Rose when we step back and take in everything we accomplished.

"You should meet her down in the lobby and then ask if she's okay with you filming giving her the packet she thinks she's picking up for a memory video for when James visits after Christmas."

"That's a fabulous idea," I tell her.

"TRINITY, YOUR GUEST IS HERE AT RECEPTION," A VOICE COMES over my phone's intercom.

"Thank you, I'll be right down," I tell her. I grab the

release authorization and head for the front. "You must be Cassidy, I'm Trinity," I greet, holding my hand out for her to shake.

"I am," she confirms. "It is so nice to meet you, I still can't believe that you went so far out of your way to do this for James and me."

"It is my pleasure. Before I take you back to the conference room, do you mind signing a release form for the filming for both you and James. We'll need that for any footage that we take of the two of you." I explain.

"Of course," she agrees and I hand over the sheet of paper. She reads it over, then signs it.

"Thank you so much, now follow me," I tell her. I'm giddy about our surprise. We enter the conference room and I already have the packet on the table. The table with gifts is in the corner and covered by a sheet. "Have a seat, I point to two chairs by the packet of paperwork."

"I don't know why I'm so nervous," Cassidy says.

"Don't be nervous," I tell her as I open the packet. "This pass will get you into the VIP lot. Just follow the signs to the VIP lot and then show it to the security or ticket people and they'll show you where to park. Once you are in the parking lot, just follow the crowd, but the lot leads directly to the VIP entrance. Once you've entered, there will be a little desk, stop at it and check in, they'll bring the two of you down to the ice level and hand you over to me to take you guys in the back hallways where the guys are stretching out, and then onto the bench for warmups. We just need James to bring his skates and helmet for the anthem. If he wants to get fully dressed, he's welcome to, but not required," I explain.

"I'll probably just stick with the minimum. Less for us to accidentally lose, and have to carry around," Cassidy says.

"We have a place he can keep his bag during the game if that helps any, but like I said it is up to you."

"Good to know."

"And don't feel like you need to make a decision right now. You can decide that day."

"Perfect," she says.

"These badges will need to be worn at all times when you aren't on the main concourse or in your seats. Otherwise, security might get grouchy."

"Got it," she chuckles.

"As for the morning skate. Arrive here at the practice facility at nine thirty with his full gear. We'll get him back to a locker room to get dressed and hang out with the guys. They're excited to meet him," I tell her.

"That is so crazy," she says, and I notice tears welling in her eyes. I reach to the center of the table and snag a couple of the tissues from a box.

"I hope those are happy tears," I say.

"Absolutely," she confirms as she dabs at her eyes. "James is going to be beside himself. He was the most popular kid on his team when he showed them the picture of him and Damien and then showed off his signed hat. I can't even imagine what it will be like when he tells them about all of this."

"Hello, hope I didn't miss too much!" Rose says as she bounces into the room.

"I've just finished going over the packet," I explain to Rose. "Cassidy, this is Rose, she's the team owner's personal assistant." I introduce the two women.

"It is so nice to meet you," Rose greets.

"Likewise," Cassidy replies.

"After we spoke yesterday, I was talking to the owner of the team about some ideas for the clinics for kids. I told him how I got information from you and how we were in touch because of Damien running into your son. He was touched by your resilience, that he wanted to give you a little more than just a day with the team." I tell her as I stand up and walk over to the table in the corner.

I tug the sheet off and reveal the pile of wrapped presents.

Cassidy gasps, then falls forward as she sobs. "You can't be serious," she says as she stands and comes to look at the table.

"Completely serious," Rose tells her as she rubs a comforting hand on Cassidy's back. We flank either side of her as her eyes rake over everything.

"Why, why us?" she asks, obviously flabbergasted.

"Why not, you?" Rose asks her. "Sometimes an angel is sent your way. Let us be your angel for a day."

"I can never thank you enough."

"Giving your son a magical Christmas is thanks enough, then sharing him with our team is payment enough." I tell her.

"I just, I have no words." She steps forward and starts reading the tags. After looking at a few of the boxes, she realizes some have her name scrolled on them. "I don't need anything," she tries to protest.

"It's already bought, paid for, and has your name on it. Plus, you wouldn't want to get us in trouble with our boss, would you?" Rose asks her as she winks at me.

"Of course not," Cassidy says.

"Good, because it was his instruction to make sure we didn't forget you on our shopping spree."

Cassidy breaks into quiet sobs again, this time pulling both Rose a me into a huge hug.

"How about we help you get all of this down to your car?" Rose suggests.

"That would be great. Seeing as how I still have to make it into work, we better get moving."

Rose and I help her, get everything loaded. Once she's pulled away, I stand there, knowing that we just made a great impact for them, even if it only lasts for a short while, they'll always remember this.

CHAPTER 21
DAMIEN

"How was your day?" I ask Trinity over dinner.

"It was so amazing," she gushes. "I met with Cassidy today. I got to give her not only the tickets for the game, but also the gifts from Nathan."

She was so excited last night after leaving work. The way she was so animated, telling me all about her shopping trip and getting everything wrapped up with Rose, made me feel like I'd been there with them. I'm glad that I could start something like what has unfolded just by chance encounter with a young kid at a gas station.

"Glad to hear that it went so well, I bet Christmas morning is going to be amazing in their house now."

"I bet it will, she tried to object to the fact that some boxes had her name on them, but Rose and I shut that down. Told her that the items were already bought, and we couldn't take them back."

"Good thinking." We chat about the rest of our day, and the upcoming schedule for the rest of the month. We could only get a couple of days off for the holidays, so it can be a crazy time of year.

Once we're both finished eating, we clear the table

together and start working on cleaning up the kitchen together. Trinity is standing at the sink, rinsing things off for the dishwasher when I bring the last the of serving dishes over from the table. I stop behind her and move her hair from her shoulder, exposing her neck for my lips. I press a kiss to the sensitive skin just behind her ear, sucking lightly. She presses her ass against my groin and my cock swells. "You smell so good," I whisper. "I could take you right here," I say.

The plate in her hand clatters into the sink as she shivers. I turn her in my arms and cover her mouth with my own. I deepen the kiss, taking what we both need.

Trinity pushes me back, "We have to stop, we have to finish the dishes and then get to the airport in an hour," she reminds me. Her parents are flying up for a long weekend visit. It's finally time that I get to meet them.

"Fine," I drop a quick kiss to the edge of her mouth. "I'll just be extra ready to fuck you later. The question is, can you be quiet?" I step back and adjust my cock, smirking at her as she watches me. "Eyes are up here, Sweetheart." I tip her chin up, so she has to look into my eyes.

"Mmhmm," she hums. I turn her back around so she's facing the sink and set to loading the dishes she's already placed on the countertop that are ready for the dishwasher.

It only takes us ten minutes to get everything cleaned up and the dishwasher going.

"Are you ready?" I ask.

"I feel like I should be the one to ask you that." She laughs. "Are you nervous to meet my parents?"

"No Sweetheart, I'm not nervous to meet them. I have nothing to be nervous about."

"They might think that you're too old for me," she teases. Our age hardly ever comes up between the two of us, so I know she's just busting my balls.

"I'll have them charmed by the time we make it to the car," I tell her.

"I'm sure you will," she says as we pull out onto the road in my SUV. It's comfortable for four adults plus their luggage. "Their flight landed a few minutes early," Trinity says as we pull into the parking garage. She wanted to go in and meet them at the exit for security, so I pull into a parking spot and kill the engine.

"I'm sure we'll still beat them to the exit." I say as we both get out, meeting in front of the SUV. I link our fingers as we walk across the parking structure to the entrance. The place is well labeled, and we quickly find the security exit, and a place to watch and wait.

"There they are!" she says, bouncing on her toes as they walk down the hall and toward us. "Mom, Dad!" she says, excited to see them as she pulls both into her open arms.

"Missed you," I hear her dad say. I let them have their moment. I can only imagine what it must be like for them to be away from their only child.

"Mom, Dad, this is Damien, and these are my parents, Barbara and Fred," Trinity introduces all of us.

"Nice to finally meet you both in person." I shake Fred's hand, giving him a firm one, but not so hard I crush his hand. I allow Barbara to wrap me in a hug, even though I'm not a big hugger, unless the person in my arms is Trinity.

"You are so much taller than I was expecting, hard as a rock as well," Barbara says as she steps back and gives me a once over. "Nice catch," she murmurs to Trinity from the corner of her mouth.

"I'd have to agree," Trinity chuckles as she slips her hand back into mine. I drop a kiss to the crown of her head, before we lead Fred and Barbara to baggage claim.

Thankfully their bags came out quickly and we're back out to the SUV a few minutes later.

"How was the flight?" I ask once everyone is settled into a seat. Fred sat up front with me and Trinity took the back with her mom.

"Not too shabby. You didn't have to put us in first class," Fred says.

"But it was lovely, thank you," Barbara pipes up from the back seat. "I think I'm spoiled now that I know what it is like to fly that way."

"Glad I could treat the two of you," I tell them as I make my way across town and back to my place. I offered to have everyone here since my place is big enough, plus Trinity is here all the time as is. She's practically moved in without actually moving in. I should maybe ask her about that soon. No sense in her paying rent for a place she only stops at to check in and grab items she wants over here.

"Your place is gorgeous," Barbara says after Trinity finishes the tour. I help Fred take their bags to the guest room, setting them just inside the door.

"Thank you for making my baby girl so happy. I haven't seen her like this in well forever," Fred says.

"I'm the lucky one, sir. She was the breath of fresh air I needed in my life. I was a lonely bastard just moping through life the last eight years after my wife died, but Trinity has brought life back into my world that I didn't realize I was missing."

"She'll do that, nudge her way in slowly, don't even realize she's doing it until she's so far embedded until she's got you."

I chuckle at his analogy, and he isn't far off. There was absolutely something about her that I was drawn to. And not just her beauty. My subconscious must have recognized her inner beauty just as my eyes recognized her outer beauty.

Its late when we finally crawl into bed. It took a while for everyone to settle in for the night.

"They loved you," Trinity says as she curls up next to my side. I wrap an arm around her and tug her a little closer. I run my hand up underneath her thin tank-top until my hand is filled with her tits. I rub my thumb over her nipple, causing it to harden underneath my touch.

"They were nice, your dad didn't even try to kill me when he cornered me," I tell her as I chuckle, remembering our little conversation.

"He cornered you?" she asks as a moan escapes her.

"I guess cornered isn't the right word," I say as I roll her onto her back and kiss along her neck. "Expressed his appreciation for making you happy, I assured him I was the lucky one in this relationship." I say into her skin as I continue to kiss along her exposed skin, tugging the tank-top down so I can swirl my tongue around her nipples before I give each of them a good suckle.

"Fuck," she moans again as I suck a little harder.

"Quiet, Sweetheart. You don't want to wake your parents," I chide, before I dive back into bringing her immense pleasure.

"Damien," she whispers my name, so I release her nipple and look up into her lust filled eyes.

"Yes, Sweetheart" I ask.

"I need you inside me, make love to me?" she asks. I can't say no to a request like that. I slide out of the bed and drop my boxer briefs. She takes that time to pull her tank top off and loose the booty shorts she had on.

She's a wet dream brought to life, right in front of me. I take my time looking her over from the top of her head to the tips of her toes. My eyes linger on her center. I can see her swollen clit as her fingers tease at the bud between her legs.

"You enjoying yourself?" I ask, my lip pulling into a smirk.

"I'd enjoy it better if your cock was inside me."

I snap into action, kneeling on the bed, I crawl over her, hovering my body above hers. I lower my head down until our lips connect, kissing her slowly, teasing her as I do. I bring a hand to her center, taking over teasing her clit. I dip two fingers lower, sinking them into her wet opening. I slowly pump my fingers in and out, teasing her relentlessly.

"Damien." My name sounds like a whine.

"You need something Sweetheart?" I pull back and ask, knowing damn well what it is she needs.

"Your cock," she whispers as she wraps her hand around my shaft and gives it a good stroke. My eyes start to roll back in my head at the contact, the blood all rushing to that appendage as it swells and hardens.

"Fuck, yes, Sweetheart." I moan into her skin as she strokes me.

We align ourselves and I slide in until my balls clap against her ass.

"Yes," she moans and adjusts her legs, hitching them both up and over my hips. She locks her heels together behind my back, which allows me to slide in a little bit deeper.

"God damn, you feel so tight around my cock," I whisper in her ear as I start a slow, yet steady pace.

Our mutual moans fill the air as we work together to build our orgasms. She crests first, the way her walls tighten around my cock sends me over the cliff and straight into the euphoric bliss. I collapse forward, my head resting on her shoulder as I take a few minutes to enjoy the moment.

"I love you, but I really need to pee," Trinity says as she taps on my back, alerting me that I need to move.

I roll off her, my cock slipping free as I go. I watch as she quickly rolls out of bed. She reaches down with her decarded sleep tank and wipes at her inner thigh, cleaning up the evidence of our love making. There's something primal that comes over me seeing her do that. Knowing that one day hopefully my seed will do its job and give us a baby of our own to nourish and love.

I grab my briefs from the floor and slide them back on, then lay back down on the bed. I fold both arms back behind my head as I lay here staring at the ceiling as I wait for Trinity to return to bed.

"What has you thinking so hard?" Trinity asks as she slides back into bed. She's put on a clean sleep tank and booty shorts.

I roll to face her and tuck a wayward chunk of hair behind her ear. She's removed every stitch of makeup she had on today yet looks so fucking perfect as she looks at me with questioning eyes. "Move in with me," I finally say. "You're already here almost every night, so why not make this place our home?" I ask her.

Her smile is blinding as she wraps an arm around me and moves in closer. Just before her lips brush against mine, she whispers, "I'd love to."

I press my lips to hers, sealing her words with a hard kiss.

"When?" I ask when we pull away from each other.

"Is there a rush?" she asks, her voice giving off a teasing tone.

"The sooner you move in, the sooner you no longer have to pay rent on a place you aren't going to," I say, it was the only lame excuse I could think of on the fly.

"That is a good one, rent is expensive. I'll have to find out if I can get out of my lease early. It doesn't renew until late spring."

"I don't care what the penalty is, I'll pay it for you," I tell her.

"I can pay the fee, I just don't know what the process is to break it, but I can call and find out."

"Okay." I kiss her again. "Do that and then let me know when I'm needed to do the heavy lifting."

"I can't imagine moving much of my furniture here, I'll probably try to sell or donate most of it as none of it is all that expensive. I was still kind of living on a college students budget until I got my job with the Shockwaves."

"Whatever you want, we can make room for your stuff, or get rid of what I have and go buy stuff together," I offer.

"That seems wasteful. I like your stuff, so no need to change it up just for me."

"As long as it feels like home to you, that's all that matters."

"Wherever you are, feels like home."

CHAPTER 22
TRINITY

I wake up excited, it is Christmas morning and I feel like a kid again. I slide out of bed, and as quietly as I can, I head to the bathroom for a quick pit stop to relieve myself, brush my teeth and pull on a pair of sweats and sweatshirt.

I slip out of the bedroom, Damien is still fast asleep, as are my parents in the guest room down the hall. I get a pot of coffee going, along with the breakfast casserole I picked up from Kendra yesterday. She added a few specials for the holidays to her menus, and I jumped on the bandwagon. Her meals are to die for and make life so easy. I pre-heat the oven and read over the instructions on the top of the lid.

While I wait for the oven to heat up, I pull out some fruit and get it washed and cut up, adding all to a platter for breakfast.

"Good morning, dear," my mother greets as she joins me in the kitchen.

"Morning, Mom," I reply, leaning into the side hug she gives me while I'm chopping fruit.

"How'd you sleep?"

"Fantastic, I'm going to have to look at the label on that

mattress and order us one for home. It is the best bed I've ever slept on."

I chuckle, but only because I thought the same thing after sleeping over here the first few times. At first I thought it was just because I was sleeping next to Damien, but that's not the only reason I get such a good night's sleep. "I can make sure you have the company's website before you head back home."

"Thank you. Is there anything I can help with this morning?" she asks.

"I think I'm good." I nod toward the container of strawberries I'm cutting up. "I only have this package left to go," I say as I look down to see only five left in the container.

"All right," she concedes.

"Coffee is done if you want a cup," I tell her.

"Absolutely." She grabs a cup and fills it up, then adds her splash or two of cream. I finish up with the strawberries just as the oven beeps that it is done pre-heating, so I place the breakfast casserole in and set the timer for the required thirty-five minutes.

I grab my own mug from the cabinet and pour a cup of coffee. I join my mom at the counter, taking a seat as I pop a strawberry into my mouth.

"Damien seems very nice, quiet, but nice." She blows on the top of her steaming cup.

"That's a good assessment of him." I smile as I take my own sip. "He's never been anything other than respectful and kind to me. After his wife, Kelly, died, he says he changed. Became really reclusive and kind of an asshole as he grieved. Didn't do much with his teammates outside of the required events. He says that he'd finally had enough with that lifestyle and was ready to make a change, and open up more, and then we met. I can't even explain it mom, we just clicked. At first, he was just super kind. Do you remember when I had that issue with my bank card number being stolen when I was in Seattle?"

"Yes, why?" she asks.

"He was behind me in line when my card was declined. I didn't realize since I was so distracted and slightly embarrassed that my card was being declined for a drink at Starbucks. Well unbeknownst to me, he told the employee he wanted to buy my drink along with his. He brought it over to me at the table I was sitting at, even offered to cover anything else I needed while we were gone."

"Sounds like you've found yourself a real winner." Mom winks at me.

"I truly have. After that incident, he'd check in on me, help explain the game, and what was going on. It seemed like every time I turned around, he was there."

"Sounds like he's a smart man, put himself where he knew you'd be. He treats you well? The sex is good?" she asks and I almost choke on the sip of coffee I was taking. "Good sex is one of the keys to a lasting relationship, so make sure you're happy now, because that's got to last you the rest of your life."

I sit here, staring at my mother slack jawed. She's never talked to me this freely about sex. "Yeah, Mom. The sex is really damn good. I didn't know it could be that good," I find myself admitting. My cheeks are flaming red, but what the hell, I might as well be truthful.

"That's good to hear." She smirks and takes another sip of her coffee.

"Smells good out here," Damien says as he joins us. He stops to give me a kiss, "Morning, Sweetheart," he whispers against my lips before walking around to grab himself a cup of coffee. He's pulled on a pair of sleep pants and t-shirt. One that clings to his chiseled torso and arms.

"Breakfast should be ready in just a few more minutes," I tell him just as my dad comes out to join us.

"Morning everyone," he greets as he also grabs a cup of coffee.

"I figured after breakfast we could open presents," I state.

"That'd be lovely, dear," my mom says.

We all chat while we wait for the casserole to finish baking, then dive right into the hot dish.

Once everyone has full bellies, we relocate to the living room. The large tree I finally put up a little over a week ago, has presents all lined up underneath, the wrapping all matching and looking like decorations themselves.

"I love this," I say as I open a larger box. It is filled with the coat I really liked when we stopped in Colorado awhile back. The store didn't have my size, and I meant to order it online, but hadn't gotten around to it. Thankfully it hasn't been super cold yet when we've traveled, but I know it will come in handy when we head to Canada next week. "Thank you." I lean over and give Damien a kiss.

"I'm just lucky you didn't already order it yourself," Damien laughs. I was worried there for a little bit. He opens the package I handed him, turning the box over and popping the tape holding it closed. He pulls out the framed picture. It is of the two of us the night of the charity auction. I figured it would look nice displayed somewhere here.

"Aww, that's a great picture of the two of you," my mom says as she leans over to look at it. "Where was that at?"

"A hotel downtown. It was at the charity auction we went to a few weeks ago," I tell her.

Mom goes next, opening the small box that I wrapped for Damien. He insisted on buying a few things for my parents, which I thought was very thoughtful. "Oh, my," mom gasps. "This is too much, Damien," she says.

"My pleasure," he tells her. "And it's for the two of you, Trinity helped, so hopefully it's a good choice," he says.

"What is it, Barbra?" My dad asks.

"A fully paid for cruise," she says, holding up the papers I printed out showing their itinerary. She hasn't notice the pages showing the round trip flights, hotel reservations for both ends of the trip, or the pre-paid visa gift card in the box yet.

"I know you guys love cruising, so figured it was the best surprise. And it is over your anniversary in March, so gives you some time to plan excursions and such."

"Wait, are these first-class flights and hotel?" Mom gasps as she continues to look through the box.

"Sure is, everything should be taken care of, or as much as we could think of," Damien tells them.

"You really went all out." My dad chuckles.

"Got to make a good impression," Damien teases back.

"I think you've just put yourself on my wife's good list for life," Dad says.

Dad opens his gift next, and it is a pass for a golf course that isn't very far from their house. He's dabbled with playing, but would never invest in a yearly membership, so he could go whenever he wanted. Now that he's retired, I thought it would be a great gift for him.

"I'm speechless, thank you both," Dad says, almost choking up at our gifts.

The rest of the morning goes just as smoothly, we finish opening the few other presents. After the living room is cleaned up from wrapping paper and boxes, Mom borrows my laptop to pull up their cruise and they start looking at the excursion options picking a few to book. They were shocked again when they pulled the cruise information up and realize that Damien paid for them to be in one of the grand suites on the ship.

CHAPTER 23
DAMIEN

I finish taping my stick, and add it to the stand that holds all the extra sticks guys have ready to go. I check the tape on my socks and ready myself for the morning skate.

"Can I have your attention," Coach calls out as he enters the room. "I have a special guest here to join us today," he says, and I notice James step forward, a huge smile on his face. I stand up and walk over, giving him a fist bump.

"Hey, buddy, you ready for today?"

"Yes!" he exclaims and the room erupts in cheers.

"This here is James Hill. He's a friend of Damien's and will be taking morning skate with us, then be back tonight to watch warmups and stand on the line during the anthem." Coach tells the guys.

"Welcome to the team, James. I'm Ryker Jorgensen, your captain," Ryker introduces himself.

James looks up at him, shock and awe written all over his face. "Nice to meet you, sir," he finally says.

"Pleasure is all mine, you ready to hit the ice? Need any help tying your skates?" Ryker offers.

"Ian got him all set up and ready," Coach says.

"Let's go men!" Ryker calls out and everyone gets up to

head out of the locker room. As everyone passes by James, they all give him fist bumps. It's when I go to leave the room with him that I notice Trinity filming everything. I toss her a wink before I lead him down the tunnel.

Before I take the ice, I notice Cassidy is on the bench, a huge smile on her face as she sees her son in pure elation. "Good morning," I stop to say.

"Good morning, Damien, thank you again for all this. I've had one excited boy on my hands since Christmas morning," she says.

James bounces up and down next to me. "I can only imagine," I reply and chuckle at his enthusiasm. "I'd better get out there, I'll talk to you later," I tell her before taking the ice. James follows me and we skate around the perimeter of the ice, getting our legs warmed up. Coach gives us five or so minutes to do so, then blows the whistle. Everyone gathers at the center where he's standing, we listen to his instructions, then disperse and start our drills. We let James take some shifts, and Blake even lets him get a few good shots past him. The pure joy coming from this kid has all of the guys on the ice smiling and laughing right along with him.

Morning skates are never hard practices and aren't even required for everyone to show up. Coach blows his whistle after forty-five minutes and instructs everyone to hit the showers, then to get a good nap in before its time to reconvene at the arena for the game tonight. Everyone knows the drill, so this isn't anything new for us.

"I don't have a long time, but can you guys grab lunch after we're out of the locker room?" I ask Cassidy. She's still standing on the bench, watching as everyone files off the ice. James is standing next to me, his face red and sweaty just like mine.

"Oh, sure," she says, much to James's excitement.

"Perfect, I shouldn't be too long," I tell her. "I think they have a place for James to take a shower too if he wants."

"Yeah, Ian got him all set up in one of the locker rooms," she says.

"Perfect," I tell her as we make our way off.

I see Trinity standing outside the locker room, watching something on her camera screen. "Get some good footage?" I stop and ask.

"Of course." She stops the footage from playing and smiles up at me.

"I'm going to grab a quick lunch with Cassidy and James, would you like to join us?" I ask.

"I could do that," she confirms.

"Good, I'll go get cleaned up then." I drop a peck on her cheek, then turn for the locker room.

I quickly strip from my gear and get cleaned up in the shower and am back out of the locker room in twenty-five minutes.

"You are fast," Cassidy remarks.

I chuckle. "Comes from the many years of playing. When we're told the bus is leaving at ten sharp, they mean business and you'd better have your ass on that bus by nine-fifty-nine or else they'll be hell to pay," I tell her. "Plus, I didn't want you ladies to have to wait on me long."

"James is still in the locker room. We might have to send in a search party for him soon." She laughs.

"My mom used to complain about how long it would take me to get undressed when I was his age. So many distractions happening in the locker room to distract us."

"Something like that," she muses just as the door opens and James comes out. Hair still wet as it drips down his neck. "Did you even attempt to dry off your head?" Cassidy asks him.

The look of realization hitting him has me chuckling. "I knew I forgot something," he says as he runs a hand over his wet head. Cassidy rolls her eyes at him. "Kids," she huffs in a playful manner.

"I don't know if you have any kids, but its moments like this that you're humbled," she says.

"I don't, but good to know," I say.

"There's a little deli around the corner, does that work for everyone?" Trinity asks.

"Works for us," Cassidy says.

We all turn for the exit, and I slip my hand around Trinity's. The entire team now knows we're together, so she's been a little more on board with minor PDA when we're at work.

"So, the two of you are an item?" Cassidy asks as we walk around the corner.

"Yes," Trinity answers, a small smile on her lips.

"Y'all are cute together. My initial impression is that you're complete opposites, but isn't the saying opposites attract?"

"Something like that," I say as we reach the deli. I open the door, allowing the three of them to go in before me. We all stand in line, reading over the large menu board hung on the wall behind the counter.

"Hello, Damien," Bob, the owner greets me when we reach the cash register. He's used to the player all coming in at some point or another. Welcomes the business that the team brings his way with our practice facility being right next to his business.

"Afternoon, Bob, how are things going?" I ask.

"Can't complain, what can I get you today?" he asks.

We all give him our orders, and he passes over a table marker.

"Where do you want to sit?" I ask James. He walks over to a larger booth, and we all slide in. I set the table marker at the end so the staff can see it when they bring our food out.

"Thank you for lunch," Cassidy says.

"Of course. Did you have fun out there today?" I ask James.

"So much fun. You guys are fast," he says.

I chuckle. I remember the first NHL practice I attended and I thought the same damn thing. I wondered how I'd keep up with the pros.

We make small talk, and Cassidy and James tell us all about their Christmas morning. Cassidy was elated with everything that Nathan had Rose and Trinity go out and get for them.

"I don't mean to be rude, but I've got to get home for my nap. I'll see everyone later," I say as I stand up. I lean over and kiss Trinity quick. "Are you coming home before the game?" I ask.

"No, I've got some work to do this afternoon. I'll just meet you over at the rink."

"Okay, see you then," I tell her.

CHAPTER 24
TRINITY

I watch as Damien walks away, my eyes following him until he's out of the deli and no longer in my sight.

"Have the two of you been together for a long time?" Cassidy asks, pulling my attention back to the table.

"No, we just met back in September," I tell her. I realize how quickly our relationship has moved. We've only been together for a couple of months, but it sometimes feels like years.

"You'd never be able to tell with how comfortable the two of you are, it reminds me of how it was with my husband. We met, were dating the next day, engaged two months later and married six weeks after that. James came along a year after that," she says as she looks over at her son lovingly.

"Aww, sounds like a true romance."

"It was, I'll miss him every day for the rest of my life."

"You and Damien have a lot in common; his wife died in a car accident years ago. It affected him for a long time, not that it doesn't still, but the way he's explained it to me is that he's just learned to live with the pain of missing her."

"I'd have to agree. There are days that it just completely

overwhelms me, but I know I have to keep going for James. He deserves the best of me always."

"I can understand that, but it's also important that you grieve for yourself. You lost the love of your life, your partner in everything."

"Oh, trust me, I've had that conversation with my therapist many times over. I've learned ways to grieve in a way that are good for me, yet I still feel like I'm supporting him in his grief."

"That's great. So, for later today. You know where to go and when to arrive?" I ask.

"Yes, I've got the packet in the car, and we'll be there. Probably before the doors even open." Cassidy chuckles.

"Perfect, you have my cell number, so if you need anything, just call or text me."

"Sounds great, thank you again for everything. I don't know how we'd ever repay all of your kindness, Damien's kindness or the teams, but we're leaning to just accept what we're given and roll with it."

"All we ask is that you enjoy the moment," I tell her.

We finish our goodbyes and head our separate ways. I go back to my office and start editing the footage from this morning. My plan is to have a montage ready to be played by game time, then we'll add more to it from what we film this evening.

I look up at the clock on the wall and realize it is time for me to head over to the arena. I gather my things, then head for my car.

Once at the arena, I get my cameras ready. I've started setting up a video one that runs continuously to capture the guys arriving. This allows me to be in other areas and not have to sit there as they all wander in at different times since it is a home game.

The time flies by, and before I know it, I'm being called by security to let me know that Cassidy and James are here. I head to our meeting spot, arriving just as they are escorted down.

"Good to see you both again," I say. Cassidy gives me a quick hug and James a high-five. "Are you ready?' I ask them both, but mostly James.

"I don't think he sat still from the moment we left the deli until we got here." Cassidy laughs.

I laugh at how energetic James is as we stand in the hallway. "Well let's get you back with the guys," I tell them. They have the badges I gave her around their necks, and we head down the hall. After flashing the passes to security, we're allowed back into the players area.

"Wow!" James gasps as we turn a corner and find most of the guys getting stretched out or warming up by kicking around a soccer ball.

"James!" Blake calls out. "Come join us," he says. James hands his mom his jersey and takes off running to the circle of guys. I look over to find one of the camera guys that works game days capturing footage for me. I met with the team and went over what footage I was hoping to get tonight. With their help, that will be possible.

"They are so good with him," Cassidy says.

"A lot of them are dads, so good with kids."

"But it's different when it isn't your kid. And while they're at work, just goes to show how good they really are."

"Believe me when I tell you they are getting just as much out of today as James is. They enjoy giving back to the community, especially to kids."

"Is there any word on the clinics you were going to try and arrange?" Cassidy asks.

"Yes! I got in touch with the director you told me about and we're in the works to schedule some over spring break week. The team is in town, and we have a few days that will work game wise."

"That's fantastic. Do you know when the camps will be

announced, and signups will be? Also the cost?"

"They will be free to attend, and I think they plan to announce just after the first of the year, but don't hold me to that. I'm not involved with the actual planning of the camps."

"I don't know if I'd be any real help, but if they need something, I'm willing to do what I can," Cassidy offers.

"I'll let those in charge know that. I'm sure they'll need some volunteers at some point."

"I just hope signups don't fill up within minutes and I miss getting James signed up. If it's while I'm at work, I'll miss out since I'm not allowed to be on my phone outside of my break times."

We watch as James hangs out with the guys, kicking the soccer ball around, then goes though some stretches they do, all before heading into the locker room to get dressed. He follows them in and comes back out with skates and his helmet in his hands. "I convinced him not to get fully dressed. Will make getting him un-dressed and to our seats a faster process."

"Probably, I wouldn't imagine he'd want to miss much of the game."

"Not at all, and when I reminded him of that, he agreed to the bare minimum."

Cassidy and I follow him out to the players bench, where we stand and watch the guys warm up. James isn't allowed to be on the ice for the official warmups due to league rules, so that's why we're just on the bench for this.

"Holy cow, I have that guy's rookie card," James says about one of the guys on the other team.

"Did you bring any card you have of the guys?" I ask. "They'd sign them for you."

"No, I forgot them." He hangs his head in defeat.

"We'll good thing your mom has my number." I wink at him. "I'm sure I can arrange to get them from you, get them signed, and then back into your possession."

"Really?" He shoots up and wraps me in a hug.

"Really," I confirm as I pat his back.

"Hey now, you trying to steal my girlfriend from me?" Damien asks as he stands on the other side of the boards from us.

James releases me immediately. "No sir," he turns to tell him.

"Good, I don't think I could compete with you," he teases.

"I made his day by telling him I could probably pull some strings to get his cards from him to get them signed and back to him," I explain to Damien.

He skates off, needing to rejoin the guys in their warmups. Once they all start to leave, heading for the locker room, we follow suit.

"Our special guest has something to read off for you guys tonight," Coach says, then steps aside so James can step forward.

"The starting line tonight is…." he says, pausing to look up at the guys. "For your forwards, we have, your captain, Ryker Jorgensen, Aiden Fox, and Jason Soaps. On defense, we have Tristan Henderson and Damien Thompson. In net, Blake Watson!" The guys all cheer and thank him for reading off the starting lineup.

"Before you go, we've got something to present to you," Coach Jackson says, he grabs the jersey that was sitting on a stool in the corner. "A team jersey for you," Coach says as he holds up the jersey, showing off the back with Hill on the back. Everyone on the team signed it today for him.

"For me?" James asks, shocked at the special gift.

"For you." Coach chuckles. "We actually have two, one that isn't signed so you can wear it and not worry about it getting ruined, and the signed one to keep," he says then hands a bag to Cassidy. "There's even a certificate of authenticity in the bag for you," he tells her.

"Thank you so much," she replies, choking back tears.

James puts on the non-signed jersey, handing the signed one over to his mom for safe keeping.

"Thank you," he says to everyone. "This has been the best day ever. My team is going to be so jealous when I tell them all about it at practice this week." The guys all chuckle at that.

"Sounds like you'll have some bragging rights," one of the guys calls out.

James just grins big at that, and I notice Cassidy just shake her head in amusement.

"Let's get out there and play hard," Coach instructs before he leaves the room.

Once the guys take the ice again, James joins them for the anthem, then it is back off the ice and into the locker room to get his skates off and him and Cassidy head for their seats.

I take up my normal place, in one of the corners of the arena so I can get footage of goals. I switch often between ends. That way I can hopefully get our goals, but also amazing saves from our goalie.

SHOCKWAVES

I'M ALMOST ASLEEP WHEN A WARM BODY SLIDES UP BEHIND ME; Damien wraps an around me and pulls me into his embrace.

"Mmmm, you smell good," he says as he buries his nose into my neck.

"I used the new body wash you got me for Christmas," I tell him as I roll in his arms so I can face him.

"I guess I picked out a good one." He smiles before kissing me. It starts slow, but neither of us keep it that way. I hook my leg over his, bringing my center closer to his body as I attempt to rub up on him.

"Someone is ready for me," he chuckles against my lips.

"Like you're not?" I question and wrap my hand around his hard cock. "You're already naked and hard." I stroke his cock, teasing him as I do.

"Fuck," he groans into my mouth. We make out like teenagers. Feeling one another up until he rolls onto his back, taking me with him. I slide onto his cock, moaning it my own pleasure as he fills me completely.

"Ride that cock, Sweetheart," he instructs.

Damien grabs my hips, helping me to rise up and down at a fast pace. The way my orgasm builds so quickly, he must notice, because as I come up, he holds me there and I fall forward, kissing him hard. He takes over, thrusting up, hard and fast. I reach down and swirl my clit and chase my orgasm right over the edge.

Damien smacks my ass, I'm sure leaving a handprint, but I don't care as the sting sends another jolt through my body as I come hard on his dick.

"Yes, come on that cock as it fills you," he dirty talks. I love it when he talks like this, it spurs me on in the moment.

Just as I come down from my orgasm, Damien flips us, then stands at the edge of the bed, pulling me over to the edge. He slides back in, then starts his relentless rhythm. I hook my legs around his body, and he presses his thumb to my clit. "You ready to come on this cock again?" He asks and increases his thrusts. My body is strung so tight that it hits me hard. I come again on his cock, bringing his orgasm out right along with mine.

Damien collapse forward, bringing his lips to mine, he pushes his tongue into my mouth, and we duel. It is a heady feeling, kissing him passionately while his cock still pulses with his orgasm inside of me.

We both slow the kiss, pulling back when I feel him start to slide out of me. "Now that was a way to say goodnight," I say and we both chuckle.

"Hell yes it was." He grabs a washcloth and hands it to me to clean up with while he does the same. I waddle over to the bathroom and fully clean up, then join him back in bed, where we curl up together and fall asleep in mutual bliss.

CHAPTER 25
DAMIEN

"Damien, can I talk to you for a minute?" Coach asks as I exit the ice. He ran us through the ringer today during practice. We're about to hit the road for a four-game road trip, and we're up against some of the top teams in the league this season, so we've got our work cut out for us.

"Sure, what's up, coach?" I ask as I enter his office. He motions to the seat across from him. I take it but can't read his expression.

"I want to start out by saying that everything is okay." He pauses, and I can feel all the blood drain from my face.

"What the fuck are you taking about?" I grit out.

"Trinity was in an accident; she's at the hospital, but she is okay. They took her there as a precaution, not because something was seriously wrong. She's asked that you come down when you were done," he says.

My heart lurches to my throat and I feel like this is déjà vu all over again. I stand abruptly, ready to run.

"Go get your stuff off and I'll be ready with a car outside. I'll drive you there myself," he says. It's no secret what happened to Kelly, or the fact that I found out after coming off the ice from a game.

"Thanks," I tell him. I run for the locker room, throwing my gear at the equipment guys as I go. I'm in the shower within two minutes and back out in a flash. I tug on the first clean shirt, briefs, and shorts I can find in my bag. I don't really care what I'm wearing, I just need to get to her.

"Everything okay, man?" Tristan asks as I shove my feet into sandals.

"Trinity's at the hospital. Coach says she's just there for precautionary reasons, but I need to get to her man," I tell him. I lock down my emotions, not ready to release them until I see her and know firsthand that she's okay and not going to leave me. This can't fucking happen again. Not to me. I won't ever recover a second time.

"Keep me posted. We've got you, whatever you need." He says before I grab my keys and wallet and run out the door.

Just as coach promised, he's waiting outside along the curb in his car. I get in and stay silent as he drives the few miles to the hospital. He must sense my need to get inside as he pulls up to the curb at the emergency room entrance and drops me off. "I'll be in after I park," he says before I slam the door shut and run inside.

I easily spot the check in desk and run directly to it.

"Can I help you?" The middle-aged woman sitting behind it asks.

"My girlfriend, Trinity Black, is here, was in an accident," I tell her.

She clicks at her screen, and I watch as her eyes move back and forth over the screen, I'm assuming reading note in the system.

"If you can go wait by that door," she points to a door marked Authorized Personnel Only, "someone will be with you in just a moment to let you back," she instructs, then picks up the phone. I can hear her tell whomever answers that I'll be waiting for them where he told me to wait.

It feels like an hour but is probably only two minutes

before the door opens. "Mr. Thompson," the nurse says, and I step forward.

"Please call me Damien," I tell her.

"Right this way, sir. Trinity has asked for you a couple of times." My heart lurches at that, knowing that my girl needed me, and I wasn't here for her already.

We step into a room, and I see her propped up on the hospital bed. She's got her head resting on a pillow and her eyes are closed. A IV is in one arm and a blood pressure cuff on the other. "Sweetheart," I say as my eyes rake her over.

"Hi," she greets, her eyes popping open as she looks directly at me.

"Are you okay?" I rush to her side, pushing back the hair on her for head.

"Sore, but I'm good. My car is probably totaled. The truck that hit me blew through the red light; I never even saw it coming."

I blow out a huge breath that nothing appears majorly wrong. Soreness will go away on its own in a few days to a few weeks depending on how bad it is.

"Do you know how long there're going to keep you?"

"I haven't heard yet. The doctor said he was waiting on a few more tests to come back and then would be back in to talk to me and let me know if they'd keep me over night to watch for anything or let me go home."

"Okay, Coach drove me over here, so I'll let him know. I can always take an Uber back to the rink to get my car if he needs to leave before we can."

"I'm sorry," she says.

"Trinity," I gather her hands, kissing both of them before I look her directly in the eyes. "You have nothing to be sorry about. This isn't your fault."

"I know, but I can only imagine what it was like for you to be told I was in an accident when you came off the ice. That had to drag up some bad memories."

"I won't lie and say it didn't feel like déjà vu, because if fucking did. But coach started off by telling me that you were okay. I held onto that with every ounce of strength I had."

We both turn at the sound of someone rapping their knuckles against the door jam, announcing their presence. "Trinity," a middle-aged man says as he enters the room. He must recognize me as his eyes go wide for a split second.

"Dr. Harvey Rasar," the man says, holding out a hand for me to shake.

"Nice to meet you, Damien Thompson," I tell him.

"I thought that was you," he admits. "I have those results I was waiting on and based on them, I'm going to order one last test before we can let you out of here. Do I have your permission to discuss your test results with Mr. Thompson in the room?" He asks.

"Yes," she says, looking at me quickly. I squeeze her hand, then turn my attention to the doctor. He takes a seat on the stool on the other side of the bed from where I stand, still holding Trinity's hand.

"Can you confirm your last menstrual cycle start date?" He asks, looking down at the tablet in his hand.

Trinity obviously thinks back. "I can't remember the exact date, but about five weeks ago," she says.

"Are your cycles usually long?" he asks.

"Sometimes, but I've gotten them somewhat under control with birth control," she explains.

"Your bloodwork shows HCG, which indicates you're about six weeks pregnant."

"Pregnant?" Trinity says, the word coming out as a whispered question. She looks at me with worried eyes.

"Yes, so I'd like to order an ultrasound just to check and make sure you're measuring the same and to make sure I don't see any bleeding from the seatbelt cutting into you."

"Okay," she says, stunned from the news.

"I'll get that order in. Let me be the first to congratulate you both," he says. "Do either of you have any questions for me right now?"

"Everything else looked okay?" I ask.

"Yes, some minor whiplash symptoms, so she'll probably be sore for a while," he says to me, then turns to talk directly to Trinity, "Some PT might help after a few days, but a following with primary care first wouldn't be a bad idea, as well as making an appointment with your OBGYN. We'll make sure your records are sent to them to review as well."

"Thank you," she says to the doctor before he steps out of the room.

"I love you," I say before she can even think of apologizing again. "Can you believe it? We created a little miracle." I rest a hand along her lower abdomen and bring my lip to hers.

"I love you," she says when I pull back. "I had no idea," she says, a tear sliding down her cheek.

"Well, I guess this is one crazy way to find out."

She attempts to chuckle, but winces at the way her body shakes. "Ugh, that hurts."

"Try not to laugh then, just rest," I tell her as I wipe away a few more tears that have run down her cheek.

"Hello, Ms. Black, I'm here to take you to ultrasound," a cheery older woman says as she pushes a wheelchair into the room.

Trinity sits up, slinging her legs over the edge of the bed. The lady walks around and takes the blood pressure cuff off her arm, then presses a few buttons on the IV computer and unhooks the IV line that is connected to her arm. "I'll have you wait here, sir. Trinity will be back in about fifteen to twenty minutes," she says.

"Okay," I tell the lady. "Sweetheart, I'm going to pop out and talk to Brett while you're gone."

"Sounds good, can we keep the baby news to ourselves for a little while?" she asks.

"Of course," I assure her. I give her a quick kiss once she's settled in the wheelchair, then follow them out of the room. I stop at the nurse's station and make sure it is okay if I pop out to the waiting room to talk to Brett and then come back. They tell me that I just need to let the check in desk know and they can call back to have the door opened like when I first arrived.

I walk out, blowing out a huge breath. I'm going to be a father. All the excitement and worry his me at once, but I lock it all down and go to find my coach.

"How's she doing?" Brett asks as he stands.

"She's good, sore and bruised but nothing is broken. They just took her back for one last test and then plan on releasing her as long as that one is good," I say without revealing what they're doing.

He blows out a breath. "That's good to hear. I can stick around, run you home to drop Trinity off and then back to the rink to get your car. What's the status of her car?" he asks.

"She thinks its totaled, but I don't even know where it is right now. I'm sure at some towing yard."

"I'm sure the police can get you that information."

"I'll call them once we're home and see what information we can get."

"Good plan, do you need a few personal days?" he asks.

"I don't know yet, but possibly. I don't know if she should be going on the trip in a few days in her condition, but that also leaves me leaving her alone," I tell him.

"You just say the word and you can take a few personal days."

"Thanks, Coach." I look down at the time on my phone and I want to get back to the room.

"Go, I'm good out here," he says and I do just that.

I make it to the room, and Trinity is pushed back in a few minutes later. She's got a huge smile on her face. "How'd it go?" I ask.

She hands me a slip of paper, when I take it, it unravels, into a long strip of black and white pictures. I look at them, trying to decipher what exactly I'm looking at. "That's our baby," she says.

I know enough that it's an ultrasound picture, but I don't know where the fuck the baby is on it.

Once Trinity is settled back on the bed, she takes the pictures from me and points out the little baby. "Here," she says, "They said the fetus is like the size of a grain of rice, but it is measuring right at six weeks and was flickering like they wanted it to be. No signs of bleeding or any damage from the accident," she says as tears slide down her cheeks.

I kiss her, her good news washing over me. "That's the best news all day," I say against her lips.

We're still in our moment when the doctor walks back in, "Sorry to interrupt," Dr. Rasar says, "Everything is good on the ultrasound, so we're working on your discharge paperwork."

"Thank you," Trinity tells him.

"How long does she need to take it easy, and when is it okay for her to travel? We're supposed to fly out in two days."

"It's not that she can't fly, but it will be really uncomfortable to do so. My advice would be to postpone your trip if possible. Taking a week to recover wouldn't be a bad idea."

"I don't know if they'll be happy about me missing the trip," she says, and I can tell she's worried.

"You can't be serious. Coach has already said if I need to take a few personal days that I can."

"I'll have to talk to Nathan," she says.

"Okay, we can worry about that later," I tell her.

The nurse brings in the discharge paperwork, going over what the doctor already explained, but also things to look out for that would require her to return for evaluation. She went over what was safe for Trinity to take for pain and when she needs to follow up with her doctors.

"If you want to pull your car up to the entrance, we can get her out of here," the nurse says to me. I shoot Brett a text to pull up and he replies with a thumbs up.

Once home, I get her settled on the couch with a bottle of water, snack, and the remote. "Where is your cell?" I ask, realizing she hasn't had it this entire time.

"I don't really know. I haven't seen it since I was in my car."

"Okay," I say, not liking the idea she can't get ahold me of if she needs something while I'm gone.

"I'll be fine," she pats my cheek. "You won't be gone long."

"I'll be back as quickly as I can," I assure her.

"Take it easy, Trinity," Brett tells her. "We'll all be thinking of you as you recover."

"Thanks, Coach," she calls out to him.

"Call the Apple Store and get a new phone purchased, they can get it all processed while we drive over to the store and pick it up, it won't take us that much longer to swing by there," he says. I do just that and after dropping my name, I have a manager on the phone doing exactly what I need him to do. He even offers to bring it directly out to me, so I don't have to come inside the mall.

Twenty minutes later, I have the new phone in my possession, her backup ready to be restored once I get it home to her. Brett drives the few miles back to the practice facility and I run in to grab my bag that I left earlier. The place is empty, everyone having already left for the day.

"Thanks again." I stop in Brett's office doorway.

"This might be a business, but we're still family around here," he says. "We take care of our own. Remember that. If you guys need anything, just let me know."

I nod, letting him know I heard him.

"Now get out of here and back to her. She needs you more than I do right now. I'm leaving as well. Holly is waiting for me to get home so we can leave for dinner."

"Sorry to keep you," I tell him.

"Not a problem, I was where I needed to be."

I depart on that note. Headed home to my girl, my baby, my future.

CHAPTER 26
TRINITY

"WE WILL TAKE GREAT CARE OF HER WHILE YOU'RE GONE," Avery assures Damien for the hundredth time.

"I can stay home, I don't mind," he argues.

"No, the team needs you, these are important games. You'll be pissed if they lose without you." Tori says.

"Fine, but if one thing goes wrong, I want to be told immediately and I'll fly back early," Damien insists.

"We can agree to those terms," Avery and Tori both agree with him. I love how they've stepped in and are taking over.

"I'll be fine," I pipe in. "I'm feeling better already." I let the little white lie slip out. The pain is actually not better, but I know it will be, I just need a few days to rest. I didn't fight much when I was on the phone with Nathan earlier today, discussing whether I'd go on this trip or not. He insisted I take a week off and then reassess my situation. Reminded me that my recovery was more important than my job. It would be there when I back to normal.

"Are you sure?" Damien comes back over to where I'm on the couch. He's doted on me from the moment I got home from the hospital. I couldn't believe it when he came home with a new phone for me. Good thing he did, because mine was found, broken in my car. The car was determined a completely loss, so that's something else I'll have to deal with at some point.

"Yes, I'll be fine. Go and play hard. Score a goal or two for me," I tell him as I cup his cheek.

"Okay," he presses a kiss to my lips, then brings his mouth to my ear. "Call me immediately if something goes wrong with you or the baby," he says this quiet enough that no one hears him. We've decided to keep the news to ourselves until at least my first OB appointment, or maybe until the second trimester if possible.

"I will," I rub his cheek, assuring him that I won't leave him in the dark. "I love you," I say before kissing him again.

"Take good care of my girl," he says to Avery, Tori, and Kendra who are all here, along with their little ones.

"We will," they all sing-song. He grabs his bags and heads for the door.

"I didn't think we'd actually get him to leave," Tori says as she sits down on the other end of the couch. Thankfully it is a big one and everyone can comfortable sit down, even with me laid out on a portion of the sectional.

"We've got a little schedule already figured out so that you'll never be alone, that is if you're okay with the guest room being taken over," Avery asks.

"You guys really don't have to go to all this trouble. I'm sore, but I can get around on my own," I say.

"We know, but we also promise to take good care of you."

"I don't mind if the guest room is used, but let's compromise, I don't want to take you away from your own homes, how about someone just comes by during the day and evening?" I suggest.

"Maybe," Tori agrees to my suggestion.

"How about we make that decision based on how you are doing tonight?" Avery says.

"I like that idea," Kendra says.

"Okay," I agree with them.

We hang out, discussing how our Christmases went last week. I tell them all about James and Cassidy and how fun it was to bless them with everything.

"Tristan told me all about him after practice. Sounds like a good kid," Tori says.

"He is, and his mom is so nice. They've both been through so much but are resilient and that shows." I tell them their story.

"How sad," Kendra says, "I can't even imagine what it would be like to lose the love of your life and then still have to function to keep your kid going."

"I think they've kept each other going," I say.

"Whew," Avery says, shaking her head like she's shaking away the tears. "Subject change. I'm hormonal and can't think of that kind of stuff right now," she says as she rubs her little pregnant belly. They just announced they are pregnant again and are on their way to having two under two when this baby is due to arrive.

We end up turning on a cheesy Christmas movie in the hallmark channel and relaxing as the two babies take an afternoon nap.

"Why don't we order in food and watch the game together?" Tori suggests.

"I love that idea," Kendra says. The rest of us go right along with the idea and pull up an app and star figuring out what everyone wants. We end up ordering from three places, deciding to splurge and get exactly what everyone wants.

Depending on how close the away team is, will determine if the guys fly in the day of. Since they started this road trip just down in LA, they went this morning for a game tonight. After the game, they're off to Vegas for tomorrow night, then have a day off and go to Colorado, and finally up to Edmonton for a game before returning.

We turn on the game, watching our feed, which gives us

the announcers that are employees of the team. "We want to send out well wishes out to one of our own," Dave, the main TV play caller says. "Our social media manger, Trinity Black, was in an accident this week and is recovering. She normally is on the road with us, so Trinity, if you're watching from home, get better, we miss you out on the road," he says.

"Aw, Dave is such a Sweetheart," Avery says.

"He is," I confirm.

We listen as they give a run down of the matchup for tonight, going into detail why the Shockwaves are the favorited team tonight, seeing as how they are well above LA in the standings.

The game finally starts, and the guys come out, guns a blazing as they quickly take control of the game, Jason Soaps collects a rebound and taps it deep into the back of the net, putting us up on the board.

"We should have called Olivia and invited her to come hang out with us," Avery says.

"Dang it, I meant to text her," Tori says. I love how much these ladies look after one another.

"And just like that, the Shockwaves take a two-to-zero lead over LA with a goal from Damien Thompson," Dave calls from the speaker of the TV. My eyes fly to the TV and I wait for the replay to show. I completely missed the play. I watch as the puck is flung at the net and deflects right off Damien's stick and into the back of the net. He is piled on by the other guy out in the ice, congratulating him for being in the right place at the right time.

"Damn, look at him go," Tori says, leaning over to give me a high-five. "If you weren't on pain meds we'd have to pull out the old shots game," she teases.

"Shots game?" I ask, confused.

"Whenever your man scores, you take a shot," Tori explains.

"What about the girls whose men score all the time?" I ask.

"I mean, we won't make you drink until its unsafe, but most guys aren't out there scoring more than a goal or two a game. Think of how hard it is for them to get a hat trick," she says.

"I guess, sounds fun. We'll have to try it another game, maybe when everyone can participate," I suggest.

"Yes, I'm so ready for this baby to get out so I can have some wine again," Avery says.

Our food finally all arrives, and we dig in.

"With is second goal tonight, Damien Thompson, extends the Shockwaves lead," Dave says and I'm stunned he scored again. He's on fire tonight and we're only a quarter of the way into the second period. It was another deflect, him being in the right place at the right time. I can't wait until the game is over and I can talk to him, congratulate him on the amazing game. I'm so glad I insisted that he go.

"Whatever you said to him must have sparked a fire in him," Kendra says.

"I just told him to go score me a goal." I chuckle. "I didn't think that he'd actually do it, best yet, two."

"Guess you'll need to ask him to do that before every game." Tori says.

"Maybe," I say as our attention is pulled back to the TV. There is a big scuffle on the ice, guys are swinging punches at each other from both teams. You can see the frustration setting in on LA's end, so they're taking cheap shots at our players.

The refs finally get everyone pulled apart and put a few guys in their respective boxes. Damien is one of them, and when the camera shows him, I can see a small cut bleeding on his upper lip.

"He'll be okay, it's just minor," Tori says.

"Oh, I'm not worried about him. I'm more worried for the

other guy and what will happen when they're both back out on the ice together."

"Why is it so fucking hot when they fight?" Kendra asks, fanning herself.

"Girl," Tori says, "I think Aiden fighting on the ice might just be how I ended up pregnant."

I smirk at their conversation. "I guess I've never looked at the fights that way," I confess.

"That's a shame, especially with how close you are to the action," Kendra says.

"Now all I'll be able to think about during the next fight I'm present for is how hot you ladies think it is," I laugh, but have to hold a pillow to my abdomen to help with the soreness and how much it hurts to laugh.

The physicality of the game mellows slightly, that is until the last five minutes of the game. LA pulls their goalie to give them the extra player. They pelt Blake with shots, but he blocks every single one of them for a minute straight. Jason gets control of the puck and skates it out of the zone, he could easily shoot it up and toward the empty net but looks back and see's Damien coming up behind him. He passes the puck to him and Damien skates a few strides with it before he sends it flying into the empty net. His third goal tonight, a natural hat trick.

"He did it!" Avery jumps to her feet, cheering for him. We celebrate his accomplishment; I just wish I was there with him to celebrate in person.

The game ends, with a shutout for Blake and the guys all jumping onto Damien to celebrate their kick-ass game. This was the easy game of the four-game swing, but with the momentum from tonight, maybe they can take that into the next three games.

CHAPTER 27
DAMIEN

I HIT THE LOCKER ROOM AND AM DOUSED WITH COLD WATER. "Damien, Damien, Damien," my teammates chant my name as they celebrate my accomplishment. Ian hands me the three pucks from my hat trick, all wrapped with tape and the information from each goal. He snaps a few pictures of me with them and then takes them back.

"Can you text me the pictures?" I ask him.

"Sure can, also sending them to Trinity," he says. "I'm sure she'll want them for herself and to post."

"Good thinking." I slap him on the back then go back to celebrating as I get undressed. We're flying out tonight to Vegas, which thankfully isn't a very long flight.

Once I'm showered, I quickly get dressed in my suit and head for the bus. "Hey, Sweetheart," I greet her when she answers the phone.

"You were incredible tonight," she gushes. "How's your lip?"

"It's fine, how are you?" I ask. She wasn't far from my mind all night.

"I'm good, the girls just left a little bit ago. I convinced them I'd be okay overnight by myself. Figured they'd all do better sleeping in their own beds."

"I guess, keep your cell phone close by," I say.

"I'm fine, I'm not helpless." She huffs.

"I know, but I'm allowed to worry about you, it's within my rights." I remind her.

"I guess," she says, and I know she's busting my balls. "You feeling okay otherwise?" I ask. She knows exactly what I'm asking without having to spell it out.

"Yes, no nausea or anything."

"Good."

"When are you guys flying out?"

"Leaving the rink in about twenty minutes," I tell her as I look at the time. "Hopefully we'll be at the hotel no later than one."

"Are you going to morning skate?" She asks.

"Probably not to skate, just to get stretched out, maybe ride the bike for a little bit."

"Don't overdo it, you had a big night tonight."

"I'm good, Sweetheart, I've been playing like this for years," I remind her.

"I know, I just hate that I wasn't there to celebrate with you in person." I can hear her pouting through the phone.

"We can celebrate when I'm home and you're feeling better," I promise.

"I'll hold you to that," she says.

"Are you going to bed soon?"

"Yes, I just need to do my last stop in the bathroom, and then I'll be crawling into bed. I just thought of something," she says.

"What's that?"

"This will be the first time I stay here by myself."

"I guess it will be, is that weird?" I ask, "It is your home now, remember?"

"I know, just something that I thought of. I'll have so

much to catch up with Michael when they get back from their trip."

"Are you telling him?" I ask.

"I don't know. I'm not sure how I'll keep it from him. He's knows me too well, and I think will know if I'm not telling him everything."

"It's okay with me if you do," I assure her. "I'd understand if you wanted your best friend to know early."

"You're sure?" she asks.

"Of course, Sweetheart."

"Okay, then I might just tell him. Would be less stressful than trying to keep it a secret."

"Why don't you invite them to dinner once I'm back, and we can tell them together? Don't they get back around then?"

"Yeah, maybe that will work," she says.

"Perfect, now get to bed. You need sleep to recover."

"Good night, I love you," Trinity says.

"Love you too, night, Sweetheart," I tell her before we disconnect the call. I load onto the bus and take a seat, leaning my head against the head rest and closing my eyes until we arrive at the airport and it's time to move.

THE PLANE TOUCHES DOWN AS MY LEG BOUNCES UP AND DOWN. The last few days have been strange. Some parts of them have flown by, while others have drug on and on. I went so long without having someone to come home to that I never thought twice about being gone, but my first road trip away from Trinity and I'm going stir crazy. We've been spoiled with the fact that she's usually on the road with me. I've slept like shit without her in my arms each night.

"You ready to get home?" Ryker asks.

"More than ever, I imagine you are as well. How's Avery

doing with the baby on the way and handling Miles now that he's mobile?"

"Like a rockstar. She was meant to be a mother. She's so damn good at it." He gushes about his wife.

"Easier this time around, even with starting over?" I ask, since he has a teenage daughter and now a baby with another on the way.

"It's different for sure. With Ellie I wasn't around all the time, so I missed a lot. With Miles, I'm as hands on as I can be when I'm home. I will say I'm not a huge fan of the middle of the night wakeups, but that just comes with the territory. You thinking about kids?" he asks.

"Not sure, I'm getting kind of old to be stating down that road, right?" I say, not wanting to give anything away until we're ready to spill the news.

"Nah, you're not that old. Think about it, kids are great. They might drive you nuts and spend a shit ton of your money, but what else are you going to do with it?" He laughs.

"You're really convincing," I tease as we both walk out to the parking lot.

"Just think about it," he tosses out as we get into our cars that are parked next to each other.

I drive straight home. I haven't seen Trinity in six days, and I need to feel her lips on my lips as her body is pressed against me.

I unlock the deadbolt and open the door. The house is quiet, the lamp from the living room giving off the only light in the place. I drop my bags to the side and stroll over to the living room and flip the lamp off, then make my way down the hall to the bedroom. I push the door open and use the light from my phone to see to my side of the bed. I watch Trinity's sleeping form as I quickly shed my clothes, then slide under the sheet and blanket. I go directly to her, being careful since I know she's still sore from the accident.

"I'm home, Sweetheart," I whisper as I run the back of my fingers on her cheek.

"Hi," she groggily greets me, turning further into my arms. I kiss her lightly and immediately feel centered, feel like I'm home and exactly where I belong.

EPILOGUE

DAMIEN

April

I STEP OFF THE FLIGHT AND WALK ACROSS THE TARMAC AND INTO the black car that is waiting for me. The driver already has the address of where I'm headed today.

We roll down the neighborhood streets and pull into the driveway. I step out of the car and walk up the driveway, stopping to ring the doorbell.

"Hello, oh, hi Damien. Is everything okay?" Barbara asks as she welcomes me into their home.

"Everything is great, I just wanted to come have a quick visit and talk to you and Fred. Is now a good time?" I ask.

"Sure," she says. "Fred, honey, Damien is here and wants to talk to us," she calls out. "Where's Trinity?" She asks, looking behind me and at the car sitting in their driveway.

"She isn't with me; she actually doesn't know that I'm here. She thinks I'm at a meeting with my agent today. His offices are down here and not far from your house." I explain.

We take a seat in the living room, "How rude of me, can I get you something to drink?" Barbara asks.

"I'm good, but thank you," I tell her.

"What brings you down so urgently?" Fred asks.

I blow out a breath, knowing that I have a plan and I can only hope they agree with it. "You know I love your daughter. With a baby of our own on the way, I'd like to marry her, and I'd like both of your blessings to do so," I say.

Before I even get the words out, Barbara is already crying and nodding her head yes.

Frank gives me a serious look up and down before a smile splits his face giving him away. "Of course you have our blessing," Frank says. "Just a second," he says, getting up and leaving the room. He returns a few minutes later with a small ring box in his hand. "This was my grandmother's ring. It has been passed down in our family. I'd be honored if you'd take it and pass it down to Trinity. It was always her favorite piece of jewelry my mother left behind and I know she'd be shocked to have it as her own ring."

I open the box and look at the ring. It has a beautiful center stone; one I could see sitting on Trinity's hand. "Thank you, I'd be honored to give her this," I tell him.

"You might need to take it to a jeweler and have it set in another setting or at least have them check that one over to make sure it won't break," he says.

"I can do that, not a problem."

"When do you plan to propose?" Barbara asks.

"I don't have a set plan in place just yet, but soon. I'd like to get married, at least legally before the baby arrives. If Trinity wants a big formal event after that, then that's what we'll do. I don't want her to miss out on her dream wedding."

"Good call," Frank says.

I visit with them for a little bit longer but need to get back to the airport for my return flight. I booked a charter, the joys of having connections to a boss that owns his own plane that he wasn't using today.

"Keep us posted, and thanks for making the trip down

just to ask in person, it goes to show your true character." Frank

"Thank you for saying that. It only felt right," I tell them.

We wave goodbye, and I'm off and back to the airport.

Once I'm back in San Francisco, I drive straight over to the jeweler I'd already talked to once about a ring. I take the one Frank and Barbara gave me in so he can take a look at it and let me know my options.

"Damien, nice to see you again. Are you back to make a purchase?" Walt asks.

"Actually, can you look at this family ring and tell me the condition and what my options are with it." I ask as I hand over the box. He takes it out and examines it under his little magnifying glasses.

"This is quite the piece of jewelry, has a history that's for sure."

"It is my girlfriend's grandmother's ring." I explain.

"The setting is a little lose, and unfortunately not something that we can repair without possibly damaging the ring. We can take the stone out and put it into a new setting if that is something you are interested in."

"If that is what you suggest, then let's do it."

He shows me different options and that's when I decide that I just don't know what Trinity would want and an idea strikes.

"Walt, I think what I should do is propose with this ring and then bring Trinity in and let her pick the new setting. That way its exactly what she wants. I'd also hate to change out her grandmother's ring and that not be what she wants."

"Good thinking. I'll be here when you're ready," he says.

With a new plan in place, I slip the ring back into the box and into my pocket. I've got a proposal to plan.

SHOCKWAVES

I lead Trinity into the restaurant, we have the back room reserved for a baby shower and gender reveal party. I also have the ring in my pocket, and plan to drop to one knee at some point today. I figured what better day to ask her. All our family and friends will be here, so there will be lots of people around to capture the moment on video. I also have some help from Avery, Tori, and Michael.

"I'm so excited to finally find out if this little one is a boy or girl," Trinity says as she looks up at me.

"Still feeling like it's a girl?" I ask. Her motherly intuition has had her thinking girl since just after we found out we were expecting. I've had no clue. Earlier this week when we had the ultrasound, the technician wrote down the gender on a card and put it into a sealed envelope for us. We gave that to Michael and he has prepped some balloons for us to pop that are filled with confetti in either pink or blue.

"Yes." She's assertive in her answer, always has been.

"As long as he or she is healthy, I don't care one way or the other," I tell her as I kiss her lips. The door to the private room opens and we walk into the party.

"Are you ready?" Michael calls out over the microphone, getting everyone's attention. He hands both of us a pin to pop the balloons with and starts a count down. *Five – four – three – two – one.* The crowd all calls out as Trinity and I both stand there with a huge balloon above us and the pins in our hands. When they reach one, we both pop our balloons and pink confetti falls everywhere.

I swoop Trinity up into my arms, pressing my lips to hers. "You we're right all along," I tell her.

"We're having a daughter!" She cries happy tears.

I set her down on her feet, and once she's steady I drop down to one knee, holding her left hand in mine. I pull up the ring box as the room gasps.

Michael is spot on when he holds the microphone up for me, "Trinity, Sweetheart, I love you and our daughter more than I can ever express. You came into my life when I didn't know what I needed or wanted out of this life. You've given me the chance at living again, loving again. We weren't each other's firsts, but I can only hope we'll be each others lasts. Trinity Black, will you marry me?" I ask her as tears stream down her cheeks.

"Yes!" she sobs out. I slide the ring onto her finger and pull her in for a searing kiss.

"Is this my grandmothers ring?" she asks a minute later when she's actually taking a second to look at it.

"It is," I confirm. "I took it to a jeweler, and he said that the setting isn't in that good of condition. We can move the stone to a new one, or if you want to keep it in the original setting, then I'll just buy you whatever ring you want. I almost had it moved, but then thought you might get upset about that, so I wanted you to decide."

"Thank you. When and how did you get this?"

"Remember that day trip I made a few weeks ago?"

"The one with your agent?" she asks.

"Yes, except I didn't go to see him, I actually went to see your parents," I tell her all about my trip.

"I can't believe you did that."

"Anything for you, Sweetheart."

READY TO HEAD BACK TO SAN FRANCISCO? BLAKE AND RAVEN are up next in Blake - Available on your favorite platform for pre-order!

COMING SOON

To find out what's next from Samantha, please visit her website at samanthalind.com

ALSO BY SAMANTHA LIND

Indianapolis Eagles Series
Just Say Yes ~ Scoring The Player
Playing For Keeps ~ Protecting Her Heart
Against The Boards ~ The First Intermission
The Hardest Shot ~ The Game Changer
Rookie Move ~ The Final Period
Box Set 1 {Books 1-3} ~ Box Set 2 {Books 4-6}
Box Set 3 {Books 7-10}

Indianapolis Lightning Series
The Perfect Pitch ~ The Curve Ball
The Screw Ball ~ The Change Up

Lyrics & Love Series
Marry Me ~ Drunk Girl
Rumor Going 'Round ~ Just A Kiss

Standalone Titles
Tempting Tessa
Then You Came Along
When I Found You

Cocky Doc

Sweet valley, Tennessee
Nothing Bundt Love
Nothing Bundt Forever

San Francisco Shockwaves
Ryker
Aiden
Tristan
Damien
Blake

ACKNOWLEDGMENTS

H, J & E - Thank you for encouraging me to write all these stories that keep me up at night. Thank you for all the time you give me to hide away and type all the words!

Renee - I seriously couldn't do this without you! It is crazy sometimes how alike we think!

Dani - Thank you for always being there when I need someone to bounce an idea off or to calm my nerves because of something that is just a tiny issue but feels like a mountain in that moment.

My readers! You are the real MVPs here! Thank you for reading my books and loving my characters as much as I do.

xoxo,

Samantha

ABOUT THE AUTHOR

Samantha Lind is a *USA TODAY* Bestselling contemporary romance author. When she's not dreaming up new stories, she can often be found with her family, traveling, reading, watching her boys on the ice or watching her favorite professional team (Go Knights Go!).

Connect with Samantha in the following places:
www.samanthalind.com
samantha@samanthalind.com

Reader Group
Samantha Lind's Alpha Loving Ladies
Good Reads
https://goo.gl/t3R9Vm
Newsletter
https://bit.ly/FDSLNL

* 9 7 8 1 9 5 6 9 7 0 1 7 3 *